A LITTLE MAGIC

Sharon E. Heisel

Houghton Mifflin Company
Boston   1991

This book is for Bereth,
who watched over the hillside
for over fifty years.

Library of Congress Cataloging-in-Publication Data
Heisel, Sharon E.
  A little magic / Sharon E. Heisel.
    p. cm.
  Summary: Jessica and her cousin Corky, a magic enthusiast,
attempt to determine the truth behind the mysterious "ghosts"
lurking their neighborhood forest.
  ISBN 0-395-55722-4
  [1. Mystery and detective stories.] I. Title.
PZ7.H3688Li 1991   90-46341
[Fic]—dc20   CIP
                AC

Printed in the United States of America

BP 10 9 8 7 6 5 4 3 2 1

Chapter 1

"Dried squirrel bones will make you invisible."

I try to ignore my cousin Corky when he talks like that. Corky is only eight. He is also impossible.

"That's nonsense. You should be ashamed to talk such pollygobble." (Pollygobble is one of my dad's homemade words. He usually uses it when he watches the evening news.)

Corky didn't answer. He trudged along beside me, gazing at the ground in sober concentration.

"Besides, how do you expect to find dried squirrel bones, anyway?"

"That's easy. All you do is locate a dead squirrel. Then you skin it and dry the bones in the sun."

Corky always has an answer. He also has red hair and freckles. He's the kind of kid grown-ups adore, the kind who should have his picture on a Christmas card or something.

"Aunt Ruth would love a dead squirrel on the patio," I said. "She could use it to dress up the house when she has company."

"Don't be dense, Jessica." He uses my full name when he is trying to sound adult. "I'd put it on the roof."

1

I told you he's impossible.

I put up with him, though. Especially now. Last spring Uncle Bill, Corky's father, was killed in a logging accident. His truck went over a bank in a bad rainstorm, and he was thrown from the cab. He died instantly when his head hit a tree. Since then, Corky talks about superstitious nonsense all the time. Dad says he is just trying to make sense of things. Mom says I should be more sympathetic. I try.

But dried squirrel bones! Honestly!

We scuffled through the early autumn leaves between my folks' house and Aunt Ruth's, dragging our feet so we would make an absolutely maximum amount of noise. We had just come through the driest summer ever recorded in southern Oregon. Twigs cracked. Dry leaves rustled and snapped underfoot with a satisfying crunch, like potato chips.

All the while, Corky's eyes moved back and forth like the big cats in cages at the zoo, searching the ground for dead squirrels. I gave up trying to reason with him and looked for leaves to use in my science project.

Corky stopped and squinted at the sky for a moment, silently, as though his mind were far away, visiting important places without him. At last he turned a questioning look my way.

"Maybe dried skunk bones would do."

Honestly!

We didn't find any bones, squirrel or skunk, and as we approached Corky's back door, we forgot to look. Good smells coming from the house promised fresh peanut butter cookies. I was ready.

Thursday is Aunt Ruth's day off from her job at Freeman's department store. The rest of the week I have to watch Corky after school until she gets home. I like Thursdays.

Aunt Ruth was just taking a sheet of cookies out of the oven. She smiled when we entered the bright kitchen and brushed a wisp of hair from her face with the back of her hand.

"Hi, Jess. Thanks for being a dear and walking home with him."

She kissed the top of Corky's head and reached to help him take off his jacket. Corky looked grim and shook his shoulders impatiently.

"I can do it myself, Mom."

He grabbed a cookie and settled in front of the television. I don't think he saw her hurt look.

"Thanks," I said as she held the plate out to me. My aunt Ruth makes superb cookies. So I meant it when I smiled at her, but I smiled a little extra hard to make up for Corky. She took a cookie too, and we sat at the big kitchen table to chat. Aunt Ruth treats me almost like an adult.

I almost am an adult, I thought. I'll be thirteen in just eight days. A teenager!

She was reading my mind.

"A teenager. I can hardly believe the time is going so fast. Your sixth birthday party seems like it was just yesterday. Corky was just a little baby then. . . ."

She looked over to where Corky was glued to the tube, and her eyes glistened a bit too much.

I reached for another cookie.

"These are great. Would you make some for my birthday party?"

That brought her back.

"Oh, sure, honey. I'll make a double batch."

We went on like that for a while, making plans for the refreshments and what I would wear. Aunt Ruth has lots of good ideas about what colors look best.

I gave up resisting a third cookie that beckoned to me from the plate. My hand was about halfway to it when a tremendous crash from outside froze me with my arm in midair.

Aunt Ruth's head jerked up.

"What in the world was that?"

Corky had jumped from his chair like a jack-in-the-box. He rushed to the window and stared out into the dimming light. I could actually see him start to tremble.

"What is it, Corky?"

He turned a sick-looking white face to me and whispered.

"A ghost. It was a ghost."

Before he could go on, Aunt Ruth grabbed him and wrapped him in a huge hug.

"No, no, baby," she said. "There are no ghosts. It must have been a dog, or maybe a raccoon in the garbage."

"No, Mom," he said, ducking from her tight grasp. "I saw a ghost."

Chapter 2

Of course, I didn't really think Corky had seen a
ghost. But it was getting dark, and the noise could
have been made by a wild animal. We do live out in
the country, after all. We even see signs of a bear
sometimes, although I'll admit I have never actually
seen the bear itself.

Still, it doesn't hurt to be careful.

Aunt Ruth and I went out and looked around,
but we didn't see anything odd. I was happy to get
back in the bright kitchen, and I was even more
happy when I heard Mom's car pull up.

She bustled in and, somehow, brought sunshine
with her. Mom is practical and cheerful and orga-
nized. I'm not sure how she got a daughter like me,
but I'm glad she did.

"Hi, hon. Want a ride home?" she said around a
bite of cookie.

I did.

By the time she had finished the cookie and another just like it, Corky was glued to the television
again and Aunt Ruth was starting to make dinner.
The tense mood was broken, but bits of it still clung
to us. Aunt Ruth's laughter was a little too loud,
and the tight lines around her mouth looked brit-

tle. I was relieved to follow Mom out to the car.

Aunt Ruth is Mom's younger sister. They grew up on this place when it was a part of my grandparents' farm. The part of the farm on the valley floor has been sold off over the years, but Mom and Aunt Ruth each kept a parcel of land on the hillside. When they married, they built houses on the two pieces, and now they are neighbors as well as sisters.

The hillside is a pretty place. Our house looks out over the river valley. Across from us a single snow-capped mountain stands like a sentinel. Behind the house the hill rises in a series of ridges that finally blend into mountains. The hill is covered with oak and ponderosa pine, with a little madrone mixed in.

I like the madrone. It sheds its bark and keeps its leaves all winter. Dad says the madrone is an Independent Thinker.

We also have a lot of wildlife: deer, foxes, porcupines, squirrels, skunks, and, as I said, an occasional bear. Behind our property is Forest Service land, so the wild creatures have plenty of wandering space.

Living here is fun, but it used to be a lot better. With Uncle Bill gone, the whole place has an empty feeling, even though we stay extra close to Aunt Ruth and Corky. Mom says they need us nearby more than ever.

She didn't say much as she drove the half mile from Aunt Ruth's house to ours, and when she stopped the car in our driveway, she gave me a close look.

"What was wrong over there?"

I should have known she would notice.

"Oh, Corky was being impossible again. There was a loud noise outside, and when he looked out the window, he said he saw a ghost. I thought it was probably a raccoon or a stray dog, but he wouldn't listen. He upset Aunt Ruth."

Mom sighed. "Corky has a vivid imagination."

Dad was home and already had dinner started, so I set the table and Mom helped. We talked about my birthday party as we clicked the silverware into place and folded napkins.

"Have you come up with a final guest list?"

Mom thought I should invite everyone in my class. She didn't understand at all about special friends, or how some people don't fit in and would be just as happy not coming. Besides, I'm not a kid anymore. I can choose my own friends.

"I'll talk to Tiff about it tomorrow. She thinks we need an even number of boys and girls."

Actually, Tiff thought we needed just four: the two of us, Josh Miller, and Tim Glisson. I didn't even try to explain *that* to Mom.

Dad whistled as he brought in his Not-So-Famous Tuna Corn Delight. We settled down to eat.

"How's the science project?" he asked, scooping out great heaps of tuna, noodles, and corn.

Science is big on Dad's list of Important Activities

for Young People, so he listened carefully as I explained about my collection of leaves and seeds.

"There's a big sugar pine up the hill," he said. "One of those huge cones would round out your collection nicely."

"Tiff is going to come home with me tomorrow. Maybe we'll go up and look for it."

Much later that night, after I finally fell asleep, I dreamed of Corky's ghost. It skittered through towering sugar pines and dropped cones on my head. I woke with a start just before dawn, listening to its eerie howling.

Howling?

Shivers danced on the back of my neck. The sound pierced my room, over and over.

"Yowooooo, yowooooo . . ."

I sat straight up in bed. The sound was coming from the woods above the house, and it was very close.

"Yowooooo, yowooooo . . ."

Was it getting closer? Should I tell Mom and Dad? I wasn't sure my legs would hold up long enough to get me to their room. The high, mournful howl broke off, then gave way to yapping.

Coyotes.

Of course. If I had just thought about it I would have known it was coyotes all along.

I never seriously thought it could have been a ghost.

Chapter 3

"Did you hear those coyotes this morning?" Dad sounded enthusiastic. "They were having a regular convention, and right in our own back yard."

Dad usually drops Corky and me off at school. Dad is cheerful in the morning. Mom says he can't help it, but we don't need to let it depress us.

I grunted politely, so he would know I had heard him, but Corky looked really interested.

"Coyotes. I wondered what was making that noise. They sure were loud."

Dad was delighted at so much response from one of us at that hour. He held forth on The Habits of Coyotes all the rest of the way to school.

Our old pickup ground to a stop in front of John Ball Elementary School, and Corky jumped out eagerly. I wasn't sure whether he was glad to get to school or to get away from the coyote lecture. Dad kept talking as he maneuvered the truck past the big playground and the jumble of other parents dropping off other kids. The street was jammed with trucks, cars, vans, bicycles, and sleepy kids. A number of the parents waved at Dad. They recognized his truck, a classic old Chevrolet that he fusses over constantly. Finally he got to the other end of the block and pulled up in the loading zone of Branberg Middle School.

He was whistling again by then, and I was beginning to wake up enough to appreciate it. I jumped out, pretended the crowd of kids leaning on the fence wasn't there, and blew him a kiss. He rewarded me with a giant wink as he drove off.

"Jess!"

My best friend, Tiffaney Collins, rushed up. Tiff is tall and has golden hair. Mr. Stallworth, our science teacher, says we look like a set of unmatched luggage.

Tiff's eyes gleamed, and she fairly danced in her shoes.

"Guess what?"

I knew she didn't really want me to guess. She looked ready to explode with her news.

"Josh asked for my phone number!"

She described every delicious detail at least twice as we went into the building, climbed the stairs, and opened our lockers.

She got me so involved in her story that I forgot I was going to tell her about Corky and his "ghost." Anyway, I thought, maybe there really is nothing to tell.

"Oh, golly, Jess, what will I do if he actually calls me?"

That stumped me. I was hardly an expert. I would probably faint if Tim called me. I thought for a moment, then said, in my most mature voice, "Just act natural."

Silence. My words stuck in the air like little pompous balloons. They sounded stupid even to me. At first I didn't dare look at Tiff, but finally I sneaked a peek.

Sure enough, her nose was wrinkled as though she smelled liver cooking, her eyes were rolling, and she clutched her stomach with both hands as she swayed back and forth. She caught my eye, and we both broke up.

We were giggling like a couple of hyenas when Tim and Josh walked by. That just made it worse. I gasped for air and stuck my head in my locker to keep from looking at Tiff and getting started again.

A voice came toward me from the left.

"Want to buy a puppy?"

Georgette. She was standing at her locker, on the other side of mine. Georgette was okay, but I wouldn't exactly have called her a friend. I was glad, though, for an excuse to change the subject. I pulled my head out of my locker and looked at her.

"What kind?"

Georgette beamed at me and pushed her glasses up with her left thumb.

"Mostly cocker spaniel, I think. They're just about ready to leave their mom, and my father says I can keep the money if I sell them."

I was a little embarrassed when she mentioned leaving their mom. Everyone knew that Georgette's mother had walked out on their family. Her father was trying to hold everything together, but there were three younger kids, and Georgette had to do a lot of the housekeeping and watch the little ones.

No one had ever heard of a mother leaving before, and we didn't know what to say. I heard Tiff cough elaborately behind me.

"I can't have a dog. My mom's allergic. She'd have to move out," I joked.

Tiff's gasp made me realize what I had said. I wished I could just disappear, and it crossed my mind that maybe Corky's squirrel dust might have a use after all.

Georgette looked stricken. I muttered something stupid about "thanks, anyway," and let Tiff pull me into class.

Honestly!

My face was still hot when Mr. Stallworth came into the room. At least he was in a good mood.

"Now, ladies and gentlemen, you will each tell me all about your vast contribution to scientific knowledge. I hardly slept last night in anticipation. Georgette, we will begin with you."

Georgette told him she was interested in finding out how dogs inherit their color. That won her a warm smile and advice to look up some scientist named Gregor Mendel.

Mr. Stallworth liked my idea of a leaf collection, too, but he said I didn't need to bring in any poison oak leaves.

13

Tiff startled me when she said she wanted to study ghosts. I think she startled Mr. Stallworth, too.

"That could be a good project, Tiffaney, but be careful how you judge reports of ghost sightings. In science we require evidence for what we accept as true."

He gave her a smile, too.

"You are not required to bring in a ghost, though. That might be more excitement than we need."

Tim Glisson said he was going to study gold mining. His grandfather had been a prospector in this valley, so he had a chance to get lots of firsthand information. There are still plenty of old gold mines around, he told us, and some are being worked again because the price of gold has gone up.

I was impressed. I think Mr. Stallworth was, too.

"Unlike Jess and Tiffaney," he said, "Tim may bring in all the samples he finds."

He laughed at his own joke, but no one minded. When he had found out about the rest of the projects, it was time for English.

In English class I sit next to Tim. Tiff slipped me a note while Mr. Thompson was handing out our assignment.

"Just act natural," it said.

Health comes after English. Ms. Sawyer introduced our unit on drug awareness by having a guest speaker. A deputy sheriff told us that southern Oregon has become a center for marijuana growers, who, he said, were a big headache for the police;

14

they planted their crops in the national forests and booby-trapped them. Innocent hikers came across marijuana growing in the little plots and accidentally tripped the booby traps. Sometimes they got hurt; last summer a young couple was even killed.

It sounded to me a little like the old stories about bootleggers and gang wars. It was hard to imagine anything like that going on in our sleepy little valley. Some of the kids didn't take it seriously at all. They sat in the back of the room and made bad jokes during the whole talk. I could see Ms. Sawyer getting mad, so I listened as well as I could while I thought about my birthday party.

Finally it was lunchtime. Tiff and I always sit together, and today, between my party and Josh, we had plenty to talk about. We dashed out as soon as Ms. Sawyer let us go.

"Look, Jess, it's fine to invite the whole class if you are in grade school, but now you're growing up. You have a right to choose your friends and to invite anyone you want to."

Tiff had said all this before. I think she was practicing, because in November she would be thirteen, and she was trying out arguments to use on her folks.

"Besides, you're old enough to have boys at a party, and it won't be fun for the girls who aren't popular if the boys ignore them."

"You have me convinced. Now all we have to do is convince my mother."

Just then Georgette sat down beside us. Cancel talk about the party, Tiff's eyes said.

The silence grew until I was afraid Georgette would think we had been talking about her. Finally I remembered that I wanted to tell Tiff about our ghost. Surely it would be safe to talk about ghosts in front of Georgette. I dove in.

"Let me tell you about the ghost Corky saw," I said.

Their eyes grew wider as I went along, and at the end I couldn't resist adding, "At least I *think* it was a coyote."

Tiff shivered in a satisfying way, but Georgette just looked worried.

"Your uncle was killed in an accident, wasn't he? Was that Corky's dad?"

"Yes."

"It must be scary to have your dad gone. It might be hard to tell the difference between a coyote and a ghost."

Chapter 4

Tiff and I were the first ones to scramble onto the bus after school. We stowed her pack with her overnight gear under the seat and settled back. I like school fine, but I prefer weekends. With my birthday just a week away and my best friend spending the night, this promised to be a good one.

Even Corky looked cheerful as he climbed aboard at the elementary school. He plopped into one of the front seats and opened a thick red book. He didn't look up until the bus sighed to a stop at the base of our road.

The three of us jumped off the bus and started up the road through the woods. We would stop at my place to leave our books, then climb the hill above the house looking for the sugar pine, but mostly just having fun.

"Thanks, Tiff, for not minding about Corky. I don't have any choice. I have to watch him until Aunt Ruth gets home."

"I kind of like him. It's almost like having a little brother of my own."

Tiff is a good friend.

It was odd for late September, but the sunshine

still held its summer warmth. The last real rain had been at the end of May. Now, after four dry months in a row, most people were worried about forest fires. But for us that day the weather was an invitation to explore.

The road wound gently up the hill, twisting to avoid the large old oak trees that lined it on the uphill side. Below the road, my grandfather had planted different kinds of apple trees: Newtown, Winesap, Gravenstein, and even a McIntosh imported from the eastern states. Most of the fruit was green, but hanging from the McIntosh were perhaps two dozen bright red apples.

Tiff lazily reached up and picked one. She wiped the dust off on her sleeve. The apple's rich color caught the light as she took a delicate bite.

"This would be a pretty color on you," she commented, holding it up by my face. "It contrasts with your ebony hair."

Tiff wants to be a designer, and she practices using color words. I have to admit that ebony hair may be the same color as black, but it sounds more beautiful.

"I've asked for a sweater just about that shade of red for my birthday," I told her, happy that she thought it would be pretty on me. "I hope I hinted hard enough."

The apple gave way with a juicy crackle as her teeth sank into it again. Filled with late summer contentment and promise, we stayed under the tree and waited for Corky to catch up.

He had lagged behind when we started up the road. Now we watched him as he stopped to pick up something from beneath the oak trees. He inspected his find carefully, then tossed it away and repeated the whole process.

I'm used to Corky acting strangely, but this was getting embarrassing. He meandered toward us, clutching his book close to his chest and keeping up his earnest search for heaven knows what.

"Come on, Corky. What are you doing, anyway?"

He glanced up with a worried expression.

"Looking for an acorn."

"You've already found at least a dozen acorns. Are you waiting for one made of solid gold?"

"It's for luck," he said, as though that explained everything.

Then I noticed the title of his book: *Magic Charms and Potions.* That did explain everything.

"Honestly, when will you grow up?"

But Corky wasn't listening. He bent and snatched an acorn from the ground, rubbed it against his jeans, then put it in his pocket with a satisfied air.

"I wanted just the right one," he mumbled.

Then he bent over and picked up two more. He handed one to each of us without a word.

"Thanks, Corky." Tiff looked pleased. She stroked

the glossy surface and studied hers. "Coffee brown," she decided, and slipped it into her pocket.

"Thanks," I told him.

We dumped our books and Tiff's pack in my kitchen, and I grabbed a plastic bag, in case we did find some new leaf specimens. We each took a handful of dried fruit — my mom believes in healthy snacks — before we headed up the hill again. Tiff swung out with her long-legged stride, and Corky tagged along behind.

"Still looking for squirrel bones?" I asked him.

He made a face at me, but then grinned and nodded. He didn't stop searching the ground.

I've explored our hill a lot more than Corky. He's younger, and lately his mother has been especially careful to keep him close to the house. I led the way as we followed an old, overgrown road up the hill. Around 1900 the hillside was logged. The loggers in those days used horses instead of trucks, so the road is actually just a trail. But it's easier to follow than the deer trails, which are likely to take off under a low-hanging branch.

The sunshine felt good on my back, and I was just beginning to wish I had a can of pop to drink when Corky cried out from behind us.

"Hey, look at this!"

Tiff and I backtracked. Corky was about ten feet off the trail in a small, open area.

"Is it a grave?"

He was staring into a rectangular hole in the

ground, about fifteen feet long and six feet wide. His back was stiff with alarm.

"No, it's not a grave. It's a pit dug by the miners who used to prospect in these hills."

I tried to sound as though the idea of a grave was silly, but I'll admit it was the right shape, and all Corky's talk of spirits and magic was beginning to affect me.

"Besides, you can tell this is old. The sides are all caved in, and there's a tree growing in it."

He still looked doubtful, but he followed us back up the path, still poking into the brush and dawdling. I felt a flash of exasperation when he called out again.

"Jess, come take a look at this!" He was staring at something near the base of a tree. "It's an omen! It must be a sign of protection."

He knelt and picked up a single charm in the shape of a four-leaf clover. Attached to it was a bit of broken chain. The chain and charm were gold; the face of the four-leaf clover was enameled with green glass.

He held it out to me, satisfaction lifting his lips into a generous smile, and I inspected it. The chain wasn't tarnished at all. It looked as though it had been dropped that very day, or at least within the last week or two. We searched around the tree, but we couldn't find any other pieces.

Tiff admired it and passed it back to Corky.

"Four-leaf clovers are supposed to be lucky,

all right," she said. "I'll bet someone misses this."

"But who could have dropped it here?" he asked, mostly to himself.

He stuffed it into his pocket with the acorn and shrugged. "Luck brings luck."

He took off on the path, leading the way this time.

We climbed toward the crest of the first low ridge, the top of our property, and began to search for the sugar pine Dad had talked about. Instead of looking up, we searched the ground. Sugar pine cones are huge, often a foot long. I figured we would look up when we found the cones and would be staring at the tree itself.

We don't have any nearby neighbors. I've never seen a stranger in our woods, so naturally I thought we were alone. The first hint I had that we were not alone was an angry roar followed immediately by the cracking snap dry brush makes when a big animal moves through it.

Bears! I grabbed Corky. Tiff must have been thinking the same thing, because she grabbed me.

The commotion got worse. Undergrowth blocked my view, but I caught glimpses of two forms (human, thank goodness), charging down the hill. They twisted and bounded along the old logging road as though they were being chased by demons. From what I could see through the brush, they almost seemed to shimmer and dance above the ground.

Moaning and whooping, they ran. A harsh clank-ing and a strange crackling, popping sound punctuated their progress, and behind them silver streamers caught the light and reflected it in all directions.

An eerie wail came at us from the opposite direction, over the crest of the ridge. With a steady rhythm the pitch rose to a shriek, fell to a rusty groan, then rose again.

As suddenly as they had appeared, the figures were gone. The awful shrieking above us abruptly stopped. In the sudden quiet, even the birds refused to call. The three of us held on to each other. I wasn't sure if Corky and Tiff were shaking, because I was quivering like a baby rattle myself. But both of them were wide-eyed, and Corky's grip on my arm was so tight, his knuckles paled.

"What was that?" My voice quavered.

Of course Corky had an answer.

"I already told you," he said grimly. His grip on my arm grew even tighter. "It was ghosts."

Chapter 5

This time I almost believed him.

Instead of following the strange apparitions back along the road, we took a shorter, steeper trail directly down toward our house. Once I had found an old square nail on this path, the kind that was used to build miners' shacks during the late 1800s. Every time I pass that place I can't help but think about the men who searched this hill for gold.

Mom has a collection of things she found on the hillside while she was growing up: a broken pipe, a crockery jug, and some bits of Chinese pottery. They were from the last century, left behind by the Chinese laborers who came to the American West to build railroads and to work the white men's mines. Most of them hoped to save enough money to bring their families from China, or, even better, to return to China with their fortunes made.

They were not happy in America. They were lonely. They worked long hours in all kinds of weather, and then instead of sleeping, they spent more hours in their quest for gold. Many of them never saw their loved ones again. They died and were buried here in a strange land. The lucky ones had a relative or friend who would send their bones back to China, but some rested here forever.

Then I had a new idea. What if they didn't rest after all? If ghosts were anywhere, they would probably be here. I kept the thought to myself, though. It was too scary, and I needed time to get used to it.

None of us said anything as we made our way to my house. I think we were each considering what we had seen or thought we had seen. And whoever, or whatever, it was might still be nearby. We were quiet.

Finally Tiff whispered, "Do you really think they could have been ghosts?"

We had gone to collect a specimen for my science project, and it seemed as though we had collected one for hers. The idea broke me out of the pollygobble I had been thinking. I was getting as impossible as Corky!

"They must have been real people," I said. "Maybe they were the ones who lost the charm."

They certainly seemed to have run out of luck!

Dad was just driving up when we reached the back door. He could tell something was wrong right away. I'm not sure how, but he can always tell.

"Come in the house and tell me about it," he said, as he climbed out of his pickup.

25

So we did.

I was relieved when he laughed at the idea of ghosts on our hill.

"Just trespassers. It happens now and then. You probably scared them witless. They won't be back."

But he turned the charm and its bit of chain in his hand thoughtfully. Then he asked Corky to let him keep it for a while. And he didn't offer any explanation for the strange wailing we had heard.

When it was time for Aunt Ruth to get home, Tiff and I walked Corky to his house. He didn't say much, but he clutched the book of magic charms tightly, and now and again one hand reached into the pocket where his "lucky" acorn nestled.

I didn't laugh. I wouldn't have admitted it out loud, but I was sort of glad to have one, too.

At home, in my room, we munched on popcorn and spent the evening revising and re-revising the guest list for my party. We listened to tapes and decided which ones to play and when. Tiff wanted to use the upbeat songs to get things rolling and to save the romantic songs for later.

"When the lights are low," she suggested, then giggled wildly.

Honestly! I'm glad I'm not that boy crazy — yet.

We discussed what we would eat and what we would wear. I was beginning to think that thirteen was going to be a lot of fun. We didn't get much sleep.

By the time I woke up, sunlight was flooding my window and washing into the corners of my room. Sleepily, I went to pull the curtains closed.

"It could be poachers."

The unfamiliar voice startled me. Squinting against the light, I peered out into our driveway — and yelped.

"Tiff, there is the *handsomest* guy out there!"

Tiff scrambled out of bed. She stretched up and cautiously peered out over my head, then she called my yelp and raised it a shriek.

The man glanced up just as I dropped the curtain. Tiff was ecstatic. She threw herself on the bed, wrapped the covers around her, and rolled back and forth, kicking her feet.

"Oooh," she crooned. "Let my heart be still. Oooh! I'm just going to *die!*"

Sometimes Tiff overreacts.

We dressed as fast as we could, considering that we wanted to look great. Tiff made me wait while she put on lipstick and eye shadow. I was sure the guy would be gone before we got downstairs, but our luck held.

"Good morning, sleepyheads," Dad said when we appeared.

Yuk! Why do parents have to say the wrong thing at crucial moments? Tiff and I did our best to look mature.

"Good morning, Mr. Overstreet."

That was a first. I'd never heard her call Dad by his last name before.

He grinned and introduced us.

"Tiffaney and Jess, I'd like to introduce Kevin Mulloy. He works for the United States Forest Service."

Kevin. I saw Tiff's eyes brighten.

"How do you do," she said.

Her lower lip began to tremble, and I was horrified. She was going to have a giggle fit right in front of him.

"Hello," I said hastily, and grabbed Tiff's arm. "We were just going to have breakfast."

He smiled, showing incredibly white teeth, and looked at us through incredibly gorgeous brown eyes. Then he said, in an incredibly deep voice, "It's nice to meet you."

We got to the kitchen just in time. Tiff began to gasp and whiffle. I had to slam the door shut so he wouldn't hear. Then I caught the giggles from her and we collapsed together.

Eventually we calmed down enough to watch from the kitchen window as Dad and the ranger — Kevin — strolled out to a pickup with the Forest Service logo on the side. They continued their conversation, their heads down, close together, for about twenty minutes. Now and then they both looked up toward the crest of the hill. Their faces were very serious. Dad pulled the charm out of his pocket and handed it to the ranger, who studied it for a long moment before he returned it. Then he swung (incredibly gracefully) into the cab of his truck. Dad stepped back and waved. "Come back any time we can be of help," he called.

Kevin Mulloy nodded at Dad, then waved at Tiff and me as we stood staring out at him.

That was enough to set Tiff off again.

Dad seemed preoccupied when he came in. He forgot to tease Tiff about her giggles, and he hardly said a word.

"Was that about the people we ran into yesterday?" I asked.

"Yes, it was. I want you girls to be careful if you see any other strangers on this place. Don't talk to them, and let me know right away."

Mom drove up then and hooted the car horn for help with groceries. We trooped out to help her, and for a few minutes we forgot about the ranger and the ghost-people. Mom was excited about the birthday cake she had ordered for me, and the conversation turned once again to the party.

Later, after driving Tiff home, Dad and I were alone in the car.

"What's a poacher?" I asked.

He looked a little surprised, but he answered quickly enough.

"Why, it's someone who takes something that isn't his, a kind of thief. Except usually poachers take something from nature, like killing a deer out of the hunting season," he said.

"Can you poach gold?"

"Why yes, I guess you could. Since the price of gold has gone up so high, a lot of people are re-working old mines and claims. I guess some of them don't care whose land they take it from. That would be poaching."

He pulled up to a stop sign and turned to look right at me.

"Look, Jess. If you're thinking about those jerks you saw running down the hill, please forget it. Just be a little extra cautious, and don't get involved. There are some seriously weird folks out there these days. I want you to stay out of their way."

"On our place? They have no right on our land."

"Maybe not on our place. Maybe they just got a little lost," he said.

Then we were home and Mom was waving frantically from the kitchen window. She met us at the door with her purse gripped in one hand and a sweater in the other.

"Ruth just called. She sounded scared. Corky thinks he saw another ghost."

Chapter 6

When we pulled up, Aunt Ruth was waiting at the front door. She flung herself at Mom and moaned, a sort of soft, desperate sound that made me shiver. Ever since Uncle Bill's accident, Aunt Ruth has seemed especially delicate. Little things bother her a lot. Mom wrapped her arms around her sister gently, as though she were a piece of dainty crystal. Mom's voice was low and soothing.

Dad and I went to find Corky.

He sat in front of the television in the kitchen, and his eyes didn't leave the screen when we came in. We all watched as an old rancher turned to his beautiful daughter and uttered, "Who *was* that masked man?"

Honestly!

"What's going on, Corky?" Dad interrupted the old rancher. "Your mother is acting like she's the one who saw the ghosts."

Corky turned to face us then, and I was shocked at his expression. His eyes were empty, and his naturally pale skin had turned white as paper. His red hair and freckles made too much contrast with his skin. The effect was a little like a clown in white-face, but definitely not a happy clown.

His head was erect and his chin was firm — too firm. He looked fragile, as though if he spoke he might shatter into little tinkling bits and disappear.

Dad looked concerned. He squatted in front of Corky and folded Corky's white hands into his big, warm grasp. He said just two words.

"Tell me."

I held my breath, but Corky didn't shatter. His thin shoulders relaxed, just a little, and he blinked twice. Dad gently squeezed his hands and looked up into Corky's face.

"Tell me."

The chin lost its stiffness as Corky started his story. Before he was finished, the tension had left him. His voice grew stronger, and his eyes took on some of their familiar light.

"I was looking for a squirrel. I heard that the bones of a dead squirrel can make you invisible."

Here he glanced at me, as if I would testify to the truth of what he said. Luckily he didn't wait for me to say anything.

"So this morning I got up early and went up the hill. I figured if I followed the deer trails I might have more luck than if I stayed on the road. I was kind of watching for a roosting tree, where there might be owl pellets. Those have bones, but I think they're mostly mouse bones."

I tried to hide my smile at the seriousness and the discouragement in his voice. Mouse bones! He really meant this invisibility business.

Dad's face never changed. He listened to each word as if it were the most important thing he would ever hear.

"Anyway, I was in a thicket of manzanita and I was bent over, looking at the ground, when I heard this awful noise. It was a kind of shrieking.

"You know." He glanced at me. "Like we heard yesterday afternoon."

"Those were sirens, Corky," I offered. But Corky's face showed he didn't accept that explanation. I didn't blame him. I wasn't sure *I* accepted my explanation, either.

"There aren't any sirens up there, Jess. And I saw something really weird. It was tall. Lots taller than you, Uncle John. It sort of dangled like it didn't really have legs. It danced in the air."

He rocked from side to side to demonstrate a jerky dance, then grew still and said, in a hushed voice, "And it didn't really have a face, either. Just a blank place where a face should have been. And no mouth, but it made that screeching noise. And it chased me."

He took a deep breath.

"It chased me. All the way home."

I didn't have any trouble staying serious this time. Corky was convincing. Whatever it was, he had seen

33

something and it had chased him. He may be a strange little kid sometimes, but he isn't a liar. And he's not crazy, either.

"Where did it stop chasing you?" Dad asked.

Corky looked relieved. At least someone was taking him seriously. He jumped up and took Dad outside, gesturing toward the trees above the house.

I had the feeling that Corky wanted to be alone with Dad, so I decided to watch some reruns and sank into Corky's abandoned chair. When Mom and Aunt Ruth came in, I was watching Lucy and Ethel cook up a scheme to trick Ricky.

Aunt Ruth was holding her head up and trying to look composed, but the strain still showed around her eyes. When Dad and Corky came in, she grabbed Corky and hugged him hard. She stroked his face and kissed him and brushed his hair back from his eyes.

"Now we'll have no more nonsense about ghosts," she said with surprising determination in her voice. "No more."

Corky nodded, but as soon as she let him go, he shook his hair down across his eyes again.

Chapter 7

The phone was ringing when we got back home. Dad answered.

"It's for you, Jess." He held the receiver out to me.

"Oh, it's probably Tiff about the movies tonight."

Dad rolled his eyes dramatically and mouthed the word "homework." But he was smiling when he walked away.

It wasn't Tiff, though. It was Georgette.

"I've been thinking, Jess. About your cousin. The one who saw the ghosts?"

Honestly. I was beginning to wish I had kept my mouth shut about ghosts.

"What about him?"

I sounded more impatient than I meant to. But I was sick of Corky's scared looks and sick of feeling scared myself. And I had really expected Tiff to call.

"Oh. Well. It's just that I have these puppies . . . you know, I mentioned them to you the other day at school, that morning in the hall, before class . . ."

Once she got started her words tumbled to-

35

gether, as though she was in a race to get them said. But she wasn't making a lot of sense.

"I'm sorry, Georgette. I just got back from Corky's house. He thinks he's seen another one."

"Oh, gosh, Jess. That's awful. I was thinking . . . I mean it's a little like my brothers . . . I mean when my mother . . . well, anyway I just had an idea . . ."

"An idea?" I tried to sound encouraging.

"Do you think he would like to have one of my puppies? I'd be glad to give him one. It might keep him from being lonely — and keep the ghosts away."

I couldn't tell if she was joking or not about the ghosts, but the puppy sounded like a really good idea. When I asked Mom what she thought, she beamed.

"That's a fantastic idea! Just let me check with Ruth first, but I'm sure she'll say it's okay."

Ten minutes later we were on our way to Georgette's house to get the puppy.

The lawn needed mowing. Badly. The sidewalk was so littered with broken and discarded toys that you might have thought they were getting ready for a garage sale, except no one would buy the stuff! We rang the doorbell, but so much noise came from the living room that I didn't really expect anyone to hear it.

The door finally popped open, and Georgette stood before us. She wore a t-shirt and jeans. One

36

hip was thrust out, and perched on the hip as if on a rocking horse was Georgette's baby sister. Georgette wrapped one arm protectively around the baby and with the other hand she shoved her glasses up.

From behind her came the blare of a television, the sound of a dog barking, the voices of her twin brothers fighting, and the smell of burnt chili. Peering at us from beneath dull brown strands of uncombed hair, she invited us in.

The baby's face — and hair — were smeared with an orangeish goo. She grinned and gurgled something I couldn't understand. Then she held her arms up in an invitation for me to take her.

Mom pretended she didn't see me shrink away. She muttered something about my coming down with a cold and reached for the baby. Georgette let her go with a sigh of relief and turned to quiet the fight. She settled it, then led us into the kitchen to see the puppies.

The mother was a golden cocker spaniel. She gazed at us with hopeful brown eyes and wagged her tail in enthusiastic agreement as we praised the puppies. As for the puppies, they concentrated on chasing each other and tumbling across the floor. All but one. A little black male rushed toward us and danced around our feet.

"That's the one," Mom said. "That is just the dog for Corky."

I knew she was right, especially when I picked up the little creature and he showed his appreciation and joy by washing my face. His rough tongue tickled, and I laughed out loud. It must have looked pretty dumb. At least Georgette and the baby both laughed, too. Then I heard Mom say, "We expect you at Jess's birthday party next Friday, Georgette."

Luckily the puppy decided that was the moment to wriggle out of my arms to attack its brother. One of the twins in the living room made a similar decision. In the confusion of sorting out the puppies and Georgette's little brothers, I don't think anyone noticed the look on my face.

I was mad!

How could Mom invite Georgette without even asking me? Georgette wouldn't have fun. She probably didn't even own a dress to wear. She would be miserable, and it would all be Mom's fault.

And what would Tiff say?

Mom insisted on paying Georgette something for the puppy. It took forever to say goodbye and get out of there. By the time we were settled in the car, with the puppy on the seat between us, I was really steaming. Mom waved to Georgette and her family as if nothing had happened.

But when we reached the corner, she said quietly, "What's wrong, Jess?"

"You shouldn't have invited Georgette. She won't have any fun. Besides, it's my party."

"I'm sorry." She sounded genuinely surprised. "I just assumed you would want her."

"She doesn't know any of the guys, and she doesn't

know how to dress, or to act. She just won't fit in, Mom."

"Jess, I think I'm hearing pollygobble," Mom said with that "I'm being patient" note in her voice.

"We've made all kinds of plans, and now they'll be ruined." I couldn't help sounding angry, but Mom's look warned me to tone it down, so I tried. "I guess it's too late now. We can't un-invite her."

But I wished we could.

Mom was silent for the rest of the drive home. So was I. Sometimes I think we are too much alike. Dad would have argued with me — tried to convince me or at least made some stupid joke. Mom just looked grim and made me feel guilty.

But I was sure I didn't have anything to be guilty about. I was certain that Georgette would feel out of place at my party.

We stopped at home for Dad, and by the time all three of us and the puppy got to Aunt Ruth's house, I was feeling better. Delivering a puppy to an eight-year-old boy has to be fun, anywhere, any time. They let me carry him into the house.

It was love at first sight.

The little dog took one look at Corky and squirmed frantically out of my arms. Corky was squirming, too. His face was as radiant as those angels you see in Christmas plays, and his freckles almost glowed with his excitement. For once, I caught a glimpse of what grown-ups see in cute little red-heads.

The puppy snuffled at Corky's pockets. Corky laughed aloud as he pulled out his lucky acorn and a battered piece of cookie that he must have been saving for an emergency. The pup made short work of the cookie, and the look he gave Corky held pure adoration. As for Corky, I hadn't seen him look so pleased since before Uncle Bill died.

Maybe Georgette was right. Maybe this would take his mind off ghosts and magic spells.

Aunt Ruth looked pleased, too. "What are you going to name him?"

Corky cocked his head and studied the little dog. The dog looked back, cocking his head in turn, as though waiting to hear his new name. I swear he was grinning.

For a moment the pair of them gazed at each other, looking like a set of bookends or a picture in one of those magazines Mom loves to read.

"I've got it!" Corky exulted. "I'll name him after the greatest wizard of all time: Merlin."

Merlin evidently liked his name. He rushed at Corky and challenged him to a game of tag. In a flurry of legs and laughter, they disappeared outside and around the corner of the house.

"Why didn't I think of this?" Aunt Ruth murmured as she watched the two of them tumble out of sight. Then she turned to Mom. "Whatever gave you such a perfect idea?"

Mom avoided my eyes when she replied, "The credit goes to Jess's friend Georgette."

Chapter 8

"Oh, Jess, NO!"

Tiff sounded outraged. Even I wasn't *that* upset.

"Well, I couldn't stop her, Tiff. And I can't ask Georgette not to come. We'll have to make the best of it."

"But we made all those plans. What if she comes in her old t-shirt and blue jeans? We'll all be embarrassed to death."

"Maybe she doesn't have anything else to wear," I offered, remembering the noisy, crowded house. Then, without much real hope, "Maybe she'll decide not to come."

"For heaven's sake, Jess, you're old enough to have all kinds of responsibilities. You take care of your cousin almost every day. Haven't you earned the right to choose your own friends?"

Before I could think of an answer, the lights dimmed and the screen brightened. Mom and Dad had agreed to my coming to the movies with Tiff, but only after I promised to spend all day Sunday on my homework.

Actually, when Dad said it, it sounded more like ALL DAY SUNDAY.

* * *

So on Sunday morning I settled down to arrange and classify my leaf and seed collection. I was sprawled on the floor with a piece of heavy cardboard, a thick black pen, and a jar of glue, trying to spell *Pinus ponderosa* (the scientific name of the ponderosa pine), when Mom knocked softly on the door.

"May I interrupt?"

"Sure." I could see "party" all over her face, so I tried a delaying tactic. "I still haven't found that sugar pine up the hill. I could sure use a cone from it."

"I can show you where it is," she said. "Let's go for a walk."

Mom knows every inch of this hillside. She grew up playing in the fields and climbing the trees. She knows where the Great Horned Owls roost, and where to find a bee tree with its store of honey. I should have realized that she could take me right to the sugar pine.

We didn't follow the old logging trail. Mom led me up paths I didn't realize went anywhere, until we reached a grove of pine trees almost at the crest of the hill. The September breeze washed across the needles with an immense sigh, and chickadees twittered in the branches of the oaks. There is no perfume on earth as sweet as the scent of pine needles and sunshine. I stopped to breathe it in.

"There," Mom said, and pointed.

The sugar pine was not any bigger than the tall ponderosa pines around it, but against the sky I could see that its needles grew in shorter tufts. Still, I might never have noticed it. When I looked down I saw the huge cones Dad had described.

"Thanks, Mom."

I picked up three cones. One of them was at least a foot and a half long! Then I stretched up to break off a twig with its cluster of five little needles. Mom watched me from a sunny spot where she sat with her back against a tall ponderosa; her hands trailed through the rust-colored needles on the forest floor.

It was impossible at that moment to believe that ghosts, or any other evil thing, might lurk nearby.

"You could use a little knife to cut those with," she remarked.

The twig broke free, and I put it with the cones in a plastic bag, then sat down, cross-legged, beside her. For a moment the only human sound was the drone of an airplane circling overhead.

"Want to talk about it?" she asked.

I did.

"Mom, I really have a lot of responsibilities. I take care of Corky nearly every day. I do my homework. I help with the chores. And by next Sunday, I'll be a teenager. I've earned some rights. Like choosing my own friends."

"You're right," she said.

That threw me.

"So why did you have to invite Georgette to my birthday party?"

"Jess, I never thought you might not want her."

43

"It's not that I don't want her. I'm just afraid she won't fit in and she'll have an awful time and be embarrassed."

"That sounds good, honey. It sounds like you really care about her."

She regarded me with a calm gaze and was silent until the silence itself began to whisper to me. Finally she sighed and patted my hand.

"Well, I'm really sorry. You're right about it being too late to un-invite her. I should have checked with you and Tiffaney. I'll remember that in the future, I promise."

"It's my choice, Mom. Tiff just talks things over with me."

Mom stood up, brushed the pine needles off the back of her pants, and reached out to help me to my feet.

"I just hope you'll let *me* talk things over with you, too."

On the way home she showed me an old dry ditch that had been dug by the Chinese laborers. The ditch had been used to carry water through sluice boxes, where the heavy gold fell out of the water and was caught on crossbars, called riffles. It was sort of a gold trap. Then the prospectors just scraped up the gold dust that the water left behind.

The workers lived there beside their "diggings," and Mom showed me the spot where she had found the pottery jug and some Chinese utensils. She told me about the old prospector who had lived on the hill before my grandparents bought it. He was called Nugget Smith. No one knew his real name. My grandfather had always said that Nugget Smith had "lost his mind searching for gold."

"Is there still gold here?"

"I suppose so, honey. If you look hard enough and have a little luck. Some people still prospect, and they seem to make a living at it. But I think the real gold on this hill is the forest and the animals."

"And the sunshine," I added.

She hugged me.

Walking with Mom in that sunshine felt good, but part of me still wondered about the possibility of ghosts. What if people were poaching gold from our hill? What if they disturbed the spirits of the Chinese miners? Maybe that was what really made Nugget Smith crazy — being chased by ghosts. Maybe they were still protecting their claim. Even the sunshine couldn't keep away the sudden chill that jolted my spine at that thought.

I forgot about ghosts, though, when we got home and smelled the appetizing aroma of Dad's Superb Sunday Brunch. He had cooked waffles and eggs and served them with spiced fresh peaches and sour cream. I ate everything but the sour cream.

Chapter 9

"Did you see a ghost?" Dad asked.

Mom smiled at him indulgently, the way she sometimes smiles at Corky.

"We didn't take time to look. We were concentrating on sugar pines and old-time prospectors."

And my party, I thought, but I decided not to bring that subject up again. After I finished my homework-a-thon (Dad's word), I called Tiff. We decided to invite Dave Gearheart to balance out the number of boys and girls, now that Georgette was coming. Dave is okay, except he laughs a little too loud whenever a teacher makes a joke. Then I sat down to write out the invitations.

     Dear _____

     You are cordually invited to help Jess Overstreet celebrate her THIRTEENTH birthday. Come to her house at 7:00 P.M. next Friday and join in the fun. No presents, please.

                          Jess

Mom approved of the invitation, especially that last part. But she made me check the spelling of "cordially."

On the way to school the next morning, Dad tried several subjects. Corky and I weren't very satisfying companions. Corky managed a few grunts, but I think he was remembering the sad look on Merlin's face when we drove off. I was thinking about the party invitations in my pack. Finally Dad gave up and switched on the radio for the morning news.

". . . still dry and unseasonably warm," the announcer stated. "Forest Service personnel predict extreme fire danger until the arrival of the fall rains, which are long overdue.

"Meanwhile, the local drug task force says that arrests are expected to pick up as the marijuana harvest moves into full swing.

"And finally, on the lighter side, a bear was tranquilized and transported to the National Forest after spending an exciting afternoon in a tree in Harry Robinson's pear orchard. Mr. Robinson called authorities when he sighted the bear early yesterday afternoon. Curious motorists stopped traffic along the Willipont Highway as they paused to wave at the bear and take pictures. Mr. Robinson —"

Dad snapped off the radio and hummed softly as he drove the rest of the way to school. When I got out of the truck, he waved and called out, "Watch out for bears!"

Honestly!

Tiff was waiting. I held out her invitation before I even said hello. She rolled her eyes at the word "cordially," but she helped me find the other kids.

Josh and Tim were playing catch with a football on the playground. Tiff giggled when I gave Josh his invitation, and I think I blushed when I gave Tim his.

I invited five other girls and six boys, including Dave Gearheart. Finally only Georgette was left.

She was staring down into her locker, wearing the same t-shirt she had been wearing last Saturday.

At least it's been washed, I thought.

"Hi, Georgette. Corky really likes the puppy. He named it Merlin."

She pushed her glasses up and stared at me. At first I thought she didn't hear, then she blinked and I realized she was trying not to cry.

Honestly! Why can't I ever say the right thing? I thrust the invitation into her hand.

She took it, looking confused, then ducked her head and read it with quick little movements of her eyes. Her hands were shaking.

When she looked up again I was horrified to see tears start to roll down her cheeks.

"Thank you, Jess. I'll be there."

Then she excused herself and was gone.

"Gosh," Tiff said in a hushed voice. "What got into her?"

We had time in Science class to work on our projects. I looked up the scientific names of sugar pines and madrone. Tiff went to the library to find books about ghosts.

"Thanks for the invitation to your party." It was Tim. "My granddad used to know an old prospector who worked your place. Nugget Smith."

"I've heard of him. They say he went crazy searching for gold."

"The gold should be there. That whole side of the valley probably has gold in it. But trying to find it can drive you crazy, all right."

"Do you think anyone is still looking?"

"Some. Mostly old-time miners."

"How about poachers?"

Tim looked interested, and suddenly it dawned on me that we were actually having a normal conversation. I pretended to write in my notebook in case I started to blush again.

"There are people around who will prospect anywhere they can, lately. I heard Granddad talking about it. They figure 'finders, keepers' no matter where they dig, I guess."

He studied me and I studied my notebook.

"What makes you ask?"

I told him about Corky and his ghosts, and about the Forest Service ranger.

"Hey, this could go in my science project. Maybe I could ask Granddad what to look for and then come up to see if there are any signs of prospecting."

That is how I wound up inviting Tim to my place after school the next day. Tiff could hardly believe it.

The rest of the day was just normal school. In English we started reading *Sherlock Holmes*. I wished that famous detective were around so I could invite him up to meet our "ghost." In Health, Ms. Sawyer showed us pictures of opium poppies and marijuana leaves. I wondered what Mr. Stallworth would say if those specimens appeared in my leaf collection.

At lunchtime Georgette still looked upset. She sat all by herself. I had almost decided to go over and try to cheer her up when the most amazing thing happened: Josh and Tim came to sit with Tiff and me.

We got started talking about gold poachers and ghosts, and I didn't notice when Georgette finished her sandwich and left.

After school Corky couldn't wait to get home to Merlin. He tore up the driveway and left me behind.

I daydreamed about Tim and being thirteen as I strolled through the crisp, dry leaves. The sleepy hum of a small airplane overhead provided a kind of background music to my daydreams.

Growing up was getting to be fun.

Chapter 10

The next afternoon was as crackling dry as breakfast cereal. We really did need rain. (But not until after Friday night, I hoped. Mom said we could play tapes and dance on the patio.)

Corky jumped off the bus first and started up the drive toward home and Merlin. His face was eager. I got off next and turned to wait for Tim.

Corky had teased us unmercifully on the bus. He had draped himself over the seat in front of us and blinked his eyes rapidly, making smacking sounds with his cute-little-red-haired-boy lips. I could have slugged him, except for what Dad calls Stifling Violent Impulses. In regular English, that means no slugging.

But I was saving up plenty of things to say to Corky, as soon as I got him alone.

Right away, Tim started looking around. There is a gully between our place and Aunt Ruth's. Each year, water from the spring and fall rains rushes down it. In the summer, especially this summer, it dries up.

"Gold would be carried down here by water," Tim said. "The gravel and grit in the bottom of the gully

51

might have a lot of gold dust and flecks. You might want to try panning it when the rain starts again."

I was disappointed. No one could be panning for gold in a dry year like this.

"How about nuggets?"

Tim squinted up the hill.

"Let's look around."

The road splits just past the apple trees. One branch leads to Aunt Ruth's house; the other goes to ours. By the time we reached the fork, Corky and Merlin were racing back to join us.

We veered up toward our house where Tim and I dumped our books on the kitchen table. Then the four of us (definitely including Merlin) set off to explore.

"Are you worried about the ghosts?" Tim asked Corky.

I cringed, but Corky didn't seem the least bit concerned.

"Nope. I've got this." He held out the four-leaf clover charm that Dad had returned to him. Then he dug in his pocket and brought forth his acorn and a sprig of mistletoe. "And these, and I have Merlin for protection."

He swung off ahead of us with a confident gait, and I thought how pleased Georgette would be if she could see him. Then an odd thing struck me. Georgette had somehow understood what Corky needed better than I had, and she really didn't even know him.

The woods were unusually quiet. Sometimes there are bird songs, but the ruckus Corky and Merlin were making had sent the birds for cover. The only sounds came from the two of them and a small airplane in the distance.

"These hills have plenty of gold still," Tim said. "I wouldn't be surprised if someone was after it. You and your folks are gone all day. The place is deserted. People might just be coming up here and helping themselves. But prospecting is hard work, and they would leave plenty of evidence behind. It should be easy to see where they were working."

All the while his eyes searched the hillside. Now and then he bent down and peered into the woods. Sometimes he scrambled down a slope and scratched around at the base of a shrub.

"It's a good idea to check the roots of plants near a bank cut by rushing water. Sometimes nuggets get trapped there."

When we came across an outcrop of granite veined with the whitish, glossy rock Mom calls quartz, Tim examined it closely.

"Have you ever found any big holes or pits dug around here?"

"Sure. Just up there."

I pointed toward the spot that Corky had thought was a grave. Tim quickened his stride and headed into the small clearing. He stopped abruptly at the edge of the pit.

"Wow! I've heard Granddad talk about these, but I've never seen one."

Beside the excavation was a rounded heap of dirt, obviously thrown up as the hole was dug. Time and weather had smoothed its outline until it almost seemed like a natural part of the hill. A little pine tree stood proudly, rooted in the pile of debris. Inside, a manzanita — a tall one — testified to the pit's age.

Again I was disappointed. No one had been working this recently. But Tim wasn't disappointed a bit. He whistled as he explored the sides, then he perched at the edge and dangled his feet down into the hole. It was still a good four feet deep, even after years of being filled by rain-washed dirt.

"What is it?"

"A pocket mine. Probably dug by Nugget Smith himself, but maybe even older than that. It might have been dug by the Chinese who worked these hills in the gold rush of the 1850s."

I squatted beside the little mine and caressed the earth with my hand. So long ago, men stood on this very spot, searching for gold and dreaming of home.

"Did they find gold?"

"I don't think so, or the whole area would have been mined. They just picked a spot above that quartz vein and dug. They were hoping for a richer part of the system. It doesn't look like they got much encouragement."

"But this is an old mine," I said. "I thought someone might be digging up here now."

Tim sat in the sunshine, a picture of contentment, and looked around at the trees and the blue, blue sky. His feet tapped rhythmically against the wall of the pocket mine.

"Maybe they went even higher. What's above us?"

"There's Forest Service land up there."

He brightened. "Well, maybe they just use your place for access. Let's go up and see if we can find any sign of prospecting."

But before we could get back to the main path, we heard Corky's triumphant voice. Merlin echoed his excitement, and in a moment they arrived, out of breath and sparkle-eyed.

"Look what I found!" Corky held up a tuft of fabric. "It was caught on a branch, just where I saw the thing that chased me."

He paused for a much-needed breath and lifted his chin. "See, I *told* you I saw a ghost."

Tim took the bit of cloth and examined it. He handed it to me without comment.

It was a piece of old sheet.

Corky insisted on having the cloth back and tucked it securely in his pocket. Then the three of us started for the top of the hill with Merlin alternately chasing and leading the procession.

The woods are denser over the crest of the hill, and the undergrowth is thick. The manzanita and poison oak grow even taller than Dad. We had to detour a number of times, but Merlin managed to dash under even the lowest branches. Sometimes Corky could scuttle through, too, with his back bent and his head down. Once he stopped and studied a leaf on the ground. Then he picked it up, stuffed it in his pocket, and plunged ahead, with Merlin prancing and grinning at his heels.

Finding the ghost-sheet bothered me. If not gold poachers, who or what could have chased Corky and scared him so? And why?

"Do you believe in ghosts?" I asked Tim.

"I think some places have special feelings attached to them," he said slowly, as though afraid I might laugh at him.

"This place does. I can almost hear the breath of the people who were here before: the Indians, the miners, the Chinese, Nugget Smith, and even my grandparents. I think they all loved this place in their own way."

I was astonished to hear myself talking so seriously to Tim about something so private. But before I had time to really analyze what I was saying, we were interrupted in the worst way possible.

We heard what sounded like a gunshot. It wasn't a BANG, but was more of a crack, like a big tree limb snapping.

Both Tim and I had heard shots before. We were

running down the hill, away from the source of the sound, before we had time to think.

"Corky!" I shouted.

Oh Lord! What if he had been shot?

"Corky!"

But there he was, running ahead of us, and the little black ball of fluff scampered behind him. Their legs were a blur. We ran, slid, leaped, flew, and skidded down the trail in a clump of pumping legs and arms. Still the shots rang out behind us, fainter now, but no less frightening.

We must have set a world record for speed getting down the hill, but to me it seemed to take forever.

We tumbled into the safety of our kitchen. I slammed the door and locked it, then sank down on the floor. Corky and Merlin crouched beside me, and Tim flopped down to join us. The shots had stopped, but we weren't going to stick our heads above window level, at least not yet.

Tim heaved a huge breath and gasped, "One thing's sure. That was *not* a ghost."

Chapter 11

Relief had filled me as I locked the kitchen door, but after sitting on the floor for a while I began to feel a little foolish. There were lots of reasons we might have heard shots up there. We had probably let our imaginations panic us. I got stiffly to my feet and was going to try to make a joke about the whole thing when I looked at Corky. I was frightened all over again.

His skin was rosy, but only a fool would say he looked healthy. The flush on his cheeks had lurid spots. There was something manic, something mad, about his eyes. He restlessly glanced around the room, as though hoping to catch some hidden creature lurking in a corner.

Tim noticed it, too. He turned on all the lights in the kitchen and whistled "Pop Goes the Weasel," a bit too loudly and off key. I was grateful for the noise.

Merlin sat as close as he could get to Corky, and I think even he looked worried. He showed no inclination to move.

"Maybe it was hunters," I offered. "The deer season is going to start. Maybe it's someone sighting his gun."

"Sure," Tim agreed, too quickly. "All this talk of ghosts and gold poachers has us spooked."

Then he looked embarrassed at his feeble joke. I was relieved when we were interrupted by the sound of Aunt Ruth driving up to get Corky.

We might have made a mistake then. Maybe we should have pretended that nothing important had happened, but I'm not sure that would have been possible.

Mothers know.

At least Aunt Ruth knew, the minute she saw Corky, that something was terribly wrong. She dropped her car keys with a clatter and rushed over to him. He didn't even try to resist when she pulled him tightly to her; then, still holding him firmly, she studied his face. I think she was seeing the same thing I had seen.

She looked frightened too.

"What happened?" she demanded. When Corky didn't respond, she turned to me, her voice rising. "What happened?"

So we told her.

When we described the shots, the color drained from her face. She embraced Corky so fiercely that I was afraid she would hurt him.

"You are never, never to go up there again," she said. Then she looked at me. "I'm sorry, Jess. I'm going to find him another babysitter for after school. I can't take any more chances."

Then with a kind of helplessness in her voice, as though she was talking to herself and no one else could understand, she said, "He's all I have."

At that, Corky stirred and tried to pull away, and spoke for the first time since our flight down the hill. "I'm okay, Mom. I have lots of protection."

Aunt Ruth thought he was talking about Merlin, but I think he meant more than that. Whatever he had in mind, it didn't make Aunt Ruth feel any better. She waited with us until Dad and Mom came home, ten minutes later. When they walked in, she was still holding Corky close.

And Corky's eyes still shifted back and forth nervously.

I had never been more glad to see my folks. By then I was really beginning to regret our panicky rush down the hill. It was probably just deer hunters preparing for the hunting season. Or maybe bird hunters. Either way, it wasn't worth Aunt Ruth getting so upset.

Dad seemed to agree with me.

"Hunters," he pronounced after listening to our foolish-sounding story. "Hunters and overbusy imaginations. But that's no reason to be careless. It would be a good idea to stick close to the house for a few weeks, until the deer season is over."

Then Tim's father arrived to pick him up, and Aunt Ruth decided to stay for dinner. Mom made her Most Delicious Meatloaf while I put together a big salad.

All the while Aunt Ruth sat at the kitchen table and chatted with us. But her eyes never left Corky.

Chapter 12

"Hunters." Tiff evidently agreed with Dad. "What else could it be, Jess? At this time of year the hunters are all over the place."

Maybe I should explain about the hunters. When deer season starts on the first weekend of October, deer hunters all head for the woods. Some of the mills even shut down. There isn't any point in staying open, because most of the men who work there are off hunting, anyway. Up in Pine Falls, the high school closes for a whole week. I guess they learned it didn't make sense to hold classes if half of the students were in the woods with their dads, chasing deer.

Lots of times you can hear shots even before the season opens as hunters adjust the sights on their guns.

Around that time we also have pheasant season. People go out in the fields and pear orchards to hunt game birds.

We don't hunt. My grandfather used to say that he quit hunting deer when he quit being hungry. But we are used to having hunters around, even though the edges of our place are posted with "No Hunting" signs.

So I told Tiff about the shots the next morning at school, but when she shrugged them off, I started to feel pretty stupid. Maybe I was letting my imagination run away with me, as Dad said. Maybe I was letting Corky and his nonsense get to me.

The thought of Corky made me a little sad, too. Aunt Ruth surely wasn't convinced that the shots had come from hunters in the woods. She had meant it when she said she'd decided to get him a "real" babysitter after school.

Last night she had called. "I need someone who can take care of him in a safe place." Her voice held apology, and I understood why when she told me who she had chosen.

Georgette!

It seemed Georgette had advertised for babysitting jobs in the paper, and Aunt Ruth recognized her name. So she called, and now Corky was to go home with Georgette instead of me. Of course, it meant less work for me, and Corky could be a pest sometimes. But Georgette! Honestly.

"Now *you're* the one talking pollygobble," Tiff said. "It's a terrific break. It means you can come to my house after school. And just think of all the free time you'll have."

She paused, gazed upward, and clutched at her heart.

63

"You might even talk Tim into exploring some old mine and get kissed in the dark."

I pretended to be exasperated, but I had to smile.

"For pity's sake, Tiff. We didn't hold hands or anything. We just tried to see if anyone had been around looking for gold." I remembered the pocket mine and added, "In the last hundred years."

It didn't calm down Tiff any when Tim picked that moment to walk up to say hi. I'm afraid I blushed.

Tiff thought that was great.

It was time for classes to start, and I knew I would have to think of something to say to Georgette. At least she seemed a little more cheerful today, so I took a chance and sat beside her in Science class.

"I hope you're not mad," she said. "Your aunt sounded really upset about having Corky at home after school. Otherwise I wouldn't have said I would take him."

"I'm not mad," I said, and when the words came out I knew they were not exactly true. I wasn't mad, but I was insulted. Didn't Aunt Ruth think I was capable of keeping an eye on an eight-year-old with a pocketful of acorns and a mind full of ghosts?

But I couldn't admit that out loud, least of all to Georgette.

"In fact, I'm glad to have him out of my hair."

It must have sounded good. Georgette looked relieved. Before I could tell any more white lies, Mr. Stallworth came in and started class.

After school I used my new freedom to go home with Tiff. She wanted to show me her new dress, and we spent the afternoon trying out hair styles. When she piles her long silky-blond hair up on top of her head, she looks at least fifteen.

Tiff has talent as well as looks. She even managed to make me look a little less like a rag doll.

"That red sweater sure would be great with your raven hair," she said as she stood back and looked me over.

We had tried a little lipstick and rouge too. She pursed her lips and squinted at me, trying to decide whether we were finished, or if we should go for the eye shadow. We decided against the shadow. My folks don't allow me to wear much make-up, and I would have to wash my face, anyway, before I went home. But she promised to come to my party early to help me get ready.

While I waited for Aunt Ruth to come for me, I was surprised to realize that I missed having Corky underfoot. I must have grown used to the little guy. When she arrived after picking up Corky, I ran down Tiff's steps and waved, giving my cheeks one last swipe with my sleeve. I got in the car and Aunt Ruth gave me an apologetic look.

"I hope you understand," she said. "I just don't want him wandering on the hillside without an adult around. And I think he really likes being with Georgette."

He certainly looked contented. He sat quietly in

the back seat, studying a small object that he held, half hidden, in his hands.

"What do you have there, Corky?"

Gently he held up a little clay doll. It was about four inches tall and had crude arms and legs. The head was large, but there was no face. Around the waist was a bit of white cloth.

With a tiny shock, I recognized the scrap of sheet he had found up the hill.

He regarded me with a bland expression. "It's a voodoo doll. For protection."

Chapter 13

I was furious with Georgette.

"How could you encourage him in that pollygobble?" I confronted her as soon as I saw her the next day.

She looked puzzled.

"Nonsense!" I shouted, realizing that she hadn't understood the word "pollygobble."

She looked more puzzled.

"Corky! How could you encourage him to make a voodoo doll?"

Understanding flooded her face.

"Jess, I think I know how he feels. He needs his magic. It makes him feel safe. I didn't think it would do any harm."

"He's obsessed with it. He actually thinks he can make himself invisible, for God's sake. He's going a little crazy, and you're helping him along!"

I was losing control. I knew I was losing control, but I couldn't stop.

Georgette nervously pushed her glasses up and peered at me with her wishy-washy brown eyes through her wishy-washy brown hair.

"I'm sorry. I'm really sorry. But it made him so happy."

Why was she so irritating? Honestly! I turned my back on her and stalked off to Science class. Tim and Josh were standing by the door staring at me, but I just lifted up my chin and marched past, pretending they weren't there.

I had a miserable day. The only thing that made me feel better was seeing Georgette look miserable too. Maybe she would learn something about taking care of eight-year-olds.

The last bell of the day rang, and I had never been so glad to hear it. By the time I got outside, Aunt Ruth and Corky were waiting. It was Thursday, Aunt Ruth's day off, and we were going to make cookies for the party.

The party. The next day it would be real, not just something to plan and dream about, but really real.

I know that dreams can be tricky. Sometimes you can spend so much time planning and hoping that when your dream finally comes, it's almost scary. What if it isn't as good as you thought it would be? What if *nothing* could be as good as you thought it would be?

All I knew that Thursday afternoon was that I was excited and scared at the same time and I wasn't sure I even wanted the birthday party anymore. I felt strange inside, jumpy. And it had nothing to do with ghosts of dead miners or Corky's superstitious nonsense. It had something to do with me, except I couldn't put words together to say exactly what.

Making the cookies helped. At least it was something I could do to occupy the time.

Aunt Ruth chatted about everyday things: the football season, her job, the long dry spell still clinging to our valley. I was happy to make small talk with her.

The only sour note was Corky. He wanted to work in the garage, putting together some kind of project, but Aunt Ruth wouldn't let him out of her sight.

"Come in here with us, Corky," she said, and when he didn't obey right away, she went to fetch him.

"You can work here, at the kitchen table. Keep us company."

She said this last lightly, with a kind of hollow cheerfulness. It sounded fine, but I had the feeling that there would be trouble if Corky refused to stay with us.

He brought in an untidy bundle of objects and spread them out on the table. He set to work, arranging and rearranging them. The red book of magic spells was open beside him, and he consulted it occasionally, then turned back to his task. He seemed to be concentrating on what he was doing, but I couldn't help thinking that he acted like a prisoner. He wanted to be somewhere else. Even Merlin seemed subdued as he settled at his master's feet.

69

Round and round I stirred the chocolate chips into a batch of cookie dough. Suddenly Corky looked up from his collection and exclaimed, "Jess!"

He startled me. I nearly dropped the spoon.

"What's wrong?"

He looked back at his collection and muttered, "Don't stir that way. It's unlucky. You should always stir clockwise."

Honestly!

So I stirred in the other direction. Anything to keep him happy. I glanced at Aunt Ruth. She shook her head in an exaggerated message of bewilderment, but I could see she was grateful to me for humoring him.

We made the chocolate chip cookies from Aunt Ruth's World Class Chocolate Chip Champion recipe. We made plain old peanut butter cookies, too, four dozen of them. We made a double batch of Golden Gem Nuggets, with apricot jam filling.

Corky was our official sampler, and that brought him out of his silence a little. He pronounced the gems good and the chocolate chip cookies outstanding.

When I gave him a plate of fresh peanut butter cookies, he was concentrating so hard that he didn't even look up. His tongue poked out of the corner of his mouth, and he breathed heavily as he wrote on a square piece of paper. The writing went around in a spiral, and he turned the paper with each word or two.

Suddenly he realized that I was there. He quickly covered the paper with his arm.

"Thanks," he muttered as he took a single cookie. He broke off a little piece for Merlin and stuffed the rest in his mouth. He declared it "vawee goob" around a mouthful of disintegrating crumbs, and went back to his work. Merlin wagged his stump of a tail. I guess he agreed with the verdict.

I believe in giving people their privacy. I would be furious if someone snooped through my things. But I couldn't stop wondering why Corky didn't want me to see what he had written. So although I'm not proud of what I did next, I'm not really sorry either. It helped me to understand what was going on with Corky, and maybe, in the end, it helped Georgette.

We were just taking the last sheet of cookies out of the oven when we heard someone drive up. Where we live, we don't get any traffic sounds. If we hear a car, we know it must be company or maybe someone looking for directions. When we heard the rough-sounding engine, Aunt Ruth left me to take the cookies off the baking sheet, while she hurried out to see who was there. At the door to the kitchen she paused, then turned to Corky.

"Come with me, honey."

Corky, looking resigned, got up and followed her out of the kitchen with Merlin making a cheerful third in the parade.

I wanted to let the cookies cool just a bit before I tried to lift them, so I set the cookie sheet on the stove. My eyes fell on the square paper that Corky had been working on so intently. I didn't think about it; I just walked over and started to read.

As I said, the words were arranged in a spiral. Corky's printing wasn't very clear, but after some deciphering I came up with this:

> Squirrel bone and tongue of bat
> Windstorm's moan and screech of cat
> By the stars and by the sea
> I invisible shall be.

I put the note down, feeling an odd mixture of confusion, frustration, and fear. Maybe I should laugh it off. Probably Corky was just going through a phase. But this phase seemed to me to be getting out of hand. While I was trying to decide how to feel about the spell, I glanced at his collection of magic charms. There was the acorn, and the little voodoo doll. (The sight of the doll irritated me all over again.) Here was the enameled four-leaf clover.

And here were some new things: a rock with a perfectly round hole through it, a small bunch of mistletoe, and a stem about six inches long with lacy leaves. The leaves spread out from the center a little like the fingers of an outstretched hand. They reminded me of something, but before I could look closer Merlin bounced in, this time at the head of the parade.

I put the cookies on the cooling rack while Aunt

Ruth returned, followed by Corky. She began to slip cool cookies into plastic bags. Her movements were tense, and she was frowning.

"Who was it?"

"Just some scruffy-looking characters. They claimed to be lost."

She sounded perturbed, almost angry. I dropped the subject. Besides, Corky had given me plenty to think about.

I thought about him again that night as I lay sleepless in bed. Aunt Ruth seemed to think his fascination with charms and amulets was just "a stage." Dad thought it was Corky's way of making himself feel safe, especially after losing his father. Georgette said Corky needed the reassurance of his magic.

But a little magic goes a long way. You have to stay connected to the real world somehow. I thought Corky's magic had gone too far. The strange events of the last few days could be meaningless, or they could be sinister. A lot depended on what you wanted them to be, and Corky seemed to want to see ghosts.

The banging outside Aunt Ruth's house last week, the figures running down the hill, the sirens, and the shots were all real. I had witnessed each one.

Mr. Stallworth said always to go for the simplest explanation, and most of those things could be simply explained. The sounds could have been made by raccoons. The figures could have been harmless trespassers, or just someone who was lost. That someone was probably also the owner of the charm. The shots could easily have been fired by hunters. That left only the sirens and Corky's bit of white sheet.

I still couldn't explain the sirens, but the bit of white sheet was easy. Corky *wanted* to see ghosts. He was the one who found the sheet, and it was just the thing a child might use to convince us, and maybe himself, that all the ghosts were real.

I had certainly been willing to be convinced. My fantasies about the Chinese miners, and even Nugget Smith, made part of me want to believe in ghosts too. But it was pollygobble. Corky's collection of charms showed how badly he was obsessed, and I had let his obsession affect me. We all had.

No more, I silently vowed. No more ghosts for me, and I'm going to do everything I can to show Corky how foolish he is being.

With that settled, I rolled over and tried to sleep. Maybe I dozed off. I was never certain afterward if what I saw was real or imaginary.

A flash of light at my window caught my attention. I thought I saw flickering lights dance up and down across my window, almost like a signal. But when I jumped out of bed to look more closely, they were gone. All was quiet. Even the coyotes refused to stir.

Feeling silly, I went back to bed and finally fell into a dream of birthdays and of being thirteen.

Chapter 14

"Calling all teenagers! Is there a teenager in the house? Front and center, all teenagers!"

I woke up the next morning with Dad's voice ringing through the house. I jumped out of bed, pulled on my robe, and opened my bedroom door.

"Happy birthday to youuu, Happy birthday to youuu . . ."

Mom and Dad stood there, each one holding a big lighted candle and singing, with more volume than tunefulness in Dad's case.

Did I mention that I love my parents?

At breakfast Dad presented me with a poor little piece of toast with thirteen birthday candles stuck into it. A beautiful box wrapped in silver paper and topped with a big red bow sat on the table. Next to it was a small, rectangular box, also wrapped in silver. Mom and Dad looked so happy, you might have thought it was their birthday, not mine.

They wanted me to open the presents. My party that evening would be for friends; this celebration was for the family.

To have your parents, both of them, to celebrate

with you is precious. I understood that then, but I understand now even more. I am lucky.

I opened the little box first. It was a special gift from Mom — a small pocketknife with a mother-of-pearl handle.

"No girl should be without one," Mom said, smiling. "You can use it for gathering specimens and for warding off ghosts."

I loved it. It was small and delicate, but the blade was sharp and strong. I slipped it into my jeans pocket.

The bigger box held my sweater. Tiff would have called it McIntosh Red, after the apple. It was a clear, bright red, true as true, red as Snow White's lips. When I tried it on I could tell by Mom and Dad's faces that it was pretty on me. The snug bands hugged my wrists and made my hands look graceful. A long look in the mirror made me almost believe that I might be pretty some day.

Gently, I took the sweater off and folded it.

Tonight, I thought. I'll wear it tonight at my party.

I left for school with a light heart.

Corky seemed content too. He wished me a happy birthday and settled in the back seat. I noticed a small leather pouch hanging from his belt.

"What's in the bag, Corky?" But I was sure I knew.

He patted it, almost the way he patted Merlin, and answered. "Magic."

That stirred up Dad. He presented us with a lecture on The Hand Is Faster Than the Eye most of the way to school. But I knew that wasn't what Corky meant. He meant it held *real* magic.

Maybe Georgette was right. Maybe it gave him some kind of comfort.

But I still thought it was pollygobble, and it had gone too far.

School was fun that day. Tiff had brought a helium balloon and tied it to my locker. Tim and Josh both threatened to spank me and give me a "pinch to grow on," but in the end they grinned and said "happy birthday." Mr. Stallworth led the class in a chorus of "Happy Birthday" that was no more tuneful than the one I had heard at home. And all day I kept thinking about my party.

If I didn't notice the sadness in Georgette's eyes, perhaps I can be excused. The only time I really saw her was at lunch. She walked up to the table where Tiff and Josh and Tim and I were eating (yes, we had been eating together all week) and she timidly held out a small package.

"Happy birthday, Jess. I hope you aren't still mad about Corky."

I didn't know what to do. It was really embarrassing to get a present from her, especially in front of the whole school. I knew she couldn't afford to buy something, but I didn't want to hurt her feelings by refusing it. I took the gift and slowly opened it.

She had made a pin using macaroni and glue. It was in the shape of a big flower, and she had painted it silver.

"I hope you like it," she said quietly. "I made it myself."

Tiff was staring at me, then at the pin. She didn't say a word. Neither did Tim or Josh. They all watched me in absolute silence. In my imagination everyone in the cafeteria watched. I'm sure I blushed.

"I love it, Georgette. It was very nice of you to remember me."

And I pinned it on my blouse.

Georgette's face flashed warmth and sweetness for a moment. Tiff looked relieved and astounded all at once. And Tim gave me a grin that was a present by itself.

Classes dragged, but finally I was on the bus, headed home. Mom was there. She was as excited as I, and we spent a giddy hour decorating.

We filled a net with balloons and hung it from the ceiling. A tug on a certain rope would spill red and blue baubles all at once into the living room. We dragged the stereo onto the patio and I arranged the tapes in order — lively at the beginning, slow at the end.

We mixed punch and arranged cookies on platters. We popped popcorn and drove to town to pick up the cake. Finally Dad came home with a bag full of burgers — our dinner — and then I went upstairs to shower and dress.

At five-thirty Tiff arrived to help me with my hair.

She squealed when she saw the sweater.

"It's gorgeous! It's perfect. You're so lucky, Jess. You look beautiful."

Maybe I did, too. Tiff fussed with my hair and made little rings of curls around my face. I certainly looked more like a girl than usual.

"One more thing," she said. "Close your eyes."

I did. I could feel Tiff brushing something on my face, and then she touched my cheeks lightly. Finally she rubbed gently on my eyelids and I could feel a brush tugging at my lashes. Then she was satisfied.

"Now," she breathed. "Look."

In the mirror I saw my eyes open, then widen. I almost believed I was looking not at myself, but at some glamorous long-lost twin.

That was the first glimpse I ever had of the woman I will someday be. I was thrilled — and a little frightened.

How would I ever get used to her? What if I did get to know her, and then she somehow vanished? Everyone would see it was only me underneath.

When I went downstairs, I think Mom and Dad saw a little of the same thing. They were utterly silent for a moment. Dad's lips tightened and he blinked. Mom pretended she had something in her eye.

There is no big and sudden change when you become a teenager. I was still me, only a day older.

I wasn't suddenly nicer or meaner or smarter or more stubborn. But I knew something for certain now that I had only dimly realized before: I was growing up, and nothing would stop it.

I felt good when the doorbell rang, and I opened it for my first guests.

Chapter 15

The party took off like a rocket. There was none of that dead time at the beginning where the guests stare and make up things to say and generally wish they had come later, or not at all. Josh and Tim were the first ones to arrive, and we were just starting the music when a whole carload of kids was dumped by someone's father. I was so busy saying hello and thank you for the happy birthday greetings that before I had time to worry about the party, it was rolling.

Aunt Ruth's cookies were a hit. The music was great. The kids talked and laughed and ate and danced. Everyone was dressed up in party clothes, and I felt wonderful in my red sweater.

Mom and Dad stayed mostly in the family room next to the kitchen. Now and then they would poke their heads out to wave and smile. Sometimes Dad brought more food or carried out empty plates, making some exaggerated reference to The Din or Adolescent Ears. I think they were having almost as much fun as I was.

Tiff looked terrific in her green dress. She called it Chinese Jade and it really seemed to make her skin and hair glow. The other girls wanted her to fix their hair, and Tiff was happy to oblige. When the girls made their entrance down the stairs, the boys pretended not to notice.

The party had been going for nearly an hour when the doorbell rang. I looked around, counting faces. Everyone was there — except Georgette. I opened the door and there she stood.

Her hair was shining, but it was as straight as ever. Her face was clean. She had on a new blouse in a pretty shade of light blue — and a brand-new pair of jeans.

I managed to blurt out, "Come in, Georgette."

It was really Mom's fault. Hadn't I warned her that Georgette would be humiliated? Suddenly, compared with Georgette's plain hair style and everyday clothes, the red sweater didn't seem cheerful; it seemed garish. Suddenly the party didn't seem like a success; it seemed like a brawl.

I stood there like a dope, blocking her way, and repeated, "Come in."

Georgette's smile faded as she walked through the living room and looked out to the patio. Three couples were dancing, and all three girls were wearing their best party dresses. One of the fellows even had on a white shirt. I could almost read Georgette's mind as she surveyed the group and realized that this was not a little kids' party. She blinked twice and her eyes were bright, but she bravely went ahead and joined two of the other girls.

Just then Tiff came down the stairs, chattering about how she wanted a full make-up kit for her thirteenth birthday. She caught sight of Georgette and stopped in mid-sentence.

I pretended not to notice and asked Tim to help me pick out the next tape. We hovered over the stereo together, and I avoided looking anywhere near Georgette. Tiff joined us.

"Didn't anyone tell her?"

Tiff sounded horrified, as if it were *my* fault that Georgette didn't know how to dress.

"It's not my fault," I snapped. The words were louder and more angry than I had intended them to be. "I didn't invite her. Mom did. I can't help it if she doesn't have a mother."

Too late, I looked up. Georgette was standing on the other side of Tim. She had heard every word.

Sometimes, when I feel especially rotten for some reason, I remember her face. It would have been less hurt if I had hit her. I hope, no matter what happens to me in my life, that I never have to see pain like that in anyone's face again.

She didn't make a sound. Like a dreamwalker, she turned and almost drifted away. With her head down she crossed the patio. She skirted a cluster of kids near the refreshment table and headed up a path through a grove of madrone trees.

I wanted to follow her, but what could I say? So far, all I had done was made things worse. Maybe it would be better for her to have a little time alone.

Besides, the light was just moving into dusk. It would be dark before very long, and she would be back.

So I didn't follow her. And I didn't tell my folks about her leaving. I didn't know how I would answer their questions about why she left, or face their eyes.

It was hard enough to face Tiff and Tim.

"Shouldn't we go after her?" Tiff really looked worried.

"No, I think she wants to be alone. I don't blame her."

I tried to sound sure of myself, but the sight of Georgette's face was too recent in my memory.

"Georgette's had a tough week," Tim said. "She heard from her mother on Monday. I guess she kept hoping her mother would come back, but . . ."

He didn't finish. He didn't need to. I felt more sick than ever. Had everyone known but me? I had been so involved with myself that I had never even asked Georgette what was wrong. Instead I had resented her for taking care of Corky and felt smug because I was nice about her present.

I wanted to throw up, or disappear. Or both.

The party dragged on. I suppose the kids had fun. I sure didn't. Then it was finally over, and cars began to pull up. Parents honked and waved or came in to say hello to Mom and Dad. Before long the driveway was empty again. I figured Georgette's dad must have come early. Maybe she had called him. I wouldn't have blamed her!

Then a rusty old station wagon banged its way up the drive. I could hear it from a long way off, and I knew before it pulled up to the house who it had to be.

The back was full with the twins and the littlest girl, and three puppies bounced on the seats as if they were trampolines.

Georgette's father had hair the same mousy brown as his daughter's, and he had the same shy smile, as if he expected to be interrupted. He climbed out of the car and one of those hopeful little smiles fluttered on his face.

"Where's Georgette?" he asked.

Chapter 16

"She left two hours ago?" Dad sounded incredulous. "Why didn't you tell us right away?"

"I thought she would come back in as soon as she felt better."

"Was she sick?" Georgette's dad blinked brown eyes behind thick lenses. His left thumb reached up, almost as if he couldn't stop it, and pushed his glasses up on his nose.

So I explained. At least I sort of explained. Georgette's father looked so hurt that I felt even worse than I had when Georgette first left.

I didn't just feel awful; I felt utterly alone.

It was certain that Mom and Dad weren't on my side. My stomach turned over when I had to tell them the story. Mom didn't look at me. Dad did, but I wished he hadn't.

I turned to Mr. Jones and tried hard not to cry. The least I could do was to act like an adult now, even if I had acted like a two-year-old earlier.

"I'm sorry. Really, really sorry. I would never have hurt Georgette on purpose. It's just that I keep saying these dumb things and . . ."

He put a gentle arm around me and gave me a

shy little hug. "It's not your fault, Jess. I'm a lousy mother, I guess. We both let Georgette down a little, but we'll do better from now on."

I did cry then.

We all jumped when the door burst open.

Mr. Jones looked up with light in his face. It must be Georgette.

But it was Aunt Ruth. She had Corky in tow and she looked furious.

"It's that babysitter, that Jones girl," she shouted. "She's been giving Corky marijuana!"

Mr. Jones's face blanched, and Dad's mouth straightened into a flat, grim line.

"Ruth," he said, "before you indulge yourself in any more pollygobble, let me introduce Georgette's father, Greg Jones."

That didn't slow down Aunt Ruth at all. Still clutching Corky's arm, she waved a bit of dried greenish stuff under Mr. Jones's nose. He drew back in alarm, and I didn't blame him. Aunt Ruth is mostly harmless, but she is a tiger where Corky is concerned, and the tiger seemed about to leap at Mr. Jones's throat.

"I found this in his bag of toys." Aunt Ruth insisted on calling Corky's charms and amulets "toys."

"It's marijuana. He must have got it from her. And I trusted that girl with my baby. I thought he would be safer with her."

Her voice rose in pitch. Each word pierced the room like a thrown knife.

Mom looked more and more alarmed and finally urged Aunt Ruth, still holding poor Corky's arm, into the kitchen.

Dad stayed with Mr. Jones. They dug out flashlights and jackets and went to search for Georgette. Luckily there was some light from the nearly full moon to help them, and to help Georgette if she was really alone out in the woods. But high clouds, the first we had seen in months, were gathering too, and they shut out some of the light. I hoped Dad and Mr. Jones would find her soon.

I was put in charge of watching Georgette's little sister and brothers. Dad admitted later that probably that had been punishment enough for me.

Much, much later I lay in my bed and tried to sort through the things that had happened that evening. Dad and Mr. Jones had not found Georgette and had finally notified the police, who advised Mr. Jones to go home in case Georgette called. They promised to come out at dawn.

"They think she may have run away." Mr. Jones hesitated and his voice dropped almost to a whisper. "You know that her mother has left. Maybe she went to find her. Anyway, they'll do what they can tomorrow."

Mr. Jones wearily urged his children into the station wagon. With a final apologetic wave, he drove off.

Meanwhile, Mom had managed to get Aunt Ruth

to settle down. Corky insisted he had "just found" the marijuana, but he refused to say any more. Each question they asked made him more stubbornly silent. I think they were becoming afraid he would withdraw completely into his private world and maybe not come out at all. Eventually they let up on him.

I had a chance to look at the marijuana. It really did look like the pictures we had seen in class. But it was so dry and the color was so dark, I wasn't surprised I hadn't recognized it when I first saw it on Aunt Ruth's kitchen table.

Still, something about it bothered me, and while I lay in bed waiting for sleep, the bothered feeling would not go away. At last I dropped off into an uneasy sleep.

I dreamed of gunshots and howling ghosts. I woke once or twice to hear the wind rushing through the tall pines around our house. Once I thought I heard crying on the hillside, but I suppose it was only coyotes.

Chapter 17

Saturday broke dull-gray and cloudy. The wind howled through the trees like a berserk flock of birds and transformed oak leaves into dervishes. The sky held no promise, only threats.

The hillside didn't seem like home at all. My secure world had changed and become something unfamiliar, even ominous. I didn't have any idea how to change it back.

If only I had kept my big mouth shut, or tried to be kind or even been polite. Just polite. It was horribly simple, the sort of thing mothers teach little children. Just be polite. In a confused way, it seemed as though I had caused all the changes with my own carelessness. I wanted to change it back by using those magic words every child knows: "I'll be good."

Corky must feel something like this, I thought. His world turned topsy-turvy when Uncle Bill died, and the only way he could think of to control it was by believing in magic.

Georgette had understood. She had tried to encourage him. But I, with my usual clumsiness, had wanted to take the magic away from him.

Corky wasn't just playing. He needed his collection of charms. He needed to feel he could disappear from all the things in his world that made him feel small.

Had he really used a drug to help him escape? I didn't think so. Still, I had heard from Ms. Sawyer that younger and younger children were turning to drugs.

A car pulled up, and I looked out to see two deputy sheriffs stride to our front door. Behind the police car rattled Mr. Jones's station wagon.

My hopes plummeted. During the night I had convinced myself that Georgette would show up at home. Now I watched with despair as the car stopped and Mr. Jones got out. His face told me that everything was *not* all right.

The wind picked at the shrubs around the door. They swayed and twisted like Corky's tall ghost.

I dressed in blue jeans and old tennis shoes, and put on a thick wool sweater. Mom's special gift, the little knife, gleamed on the dresser. On my way out of the room I picked it up and slipped it into my pocket. Maybe I could help look for Georgette.

Or maybe they would think I had already done too much.

The two deputies, Mom, Dad, and Mr. Jones had gathered in our kitchen. No one paid any attention to me when I quietly entered. One of the deputies was talking.

"Mr. Jones says he is sure his daughter wouldn't run away, but that is a possibility we are obliged to consider. We'll start searching around the house, and, if she doesn't show up this morning, we'll bring out the bloodhounds to see if we can catch a trail. Now, did anyone actually see her leave the house?"

Five pairs of eyes fell on me. No one looked stern or accusing. I might actually have felt better if they had. But Mom was sympathetic, the deputies were attentive, Dad's face was a careful blank, and Mr. Jones — well, he just looked afraid.

"We were having a party. Georgette left by the door to the patio, but there were a bunch of kids out there. So she went the other way. She wanted to get away from everyone, I guess. Anyway, she took a path up the hill."

"Why did she leave in the middle of your party?" It was the younger deputy.

"It was something I said. I hurt her feelings, even though I didn't mean to. She wasn't mad, just hurt and maybe embarrassed. We thought she would be back before dark."

The deputies spread out a map on the table and we all clustered around. Dad pointed to the path Georgette had taken.

"But she could be anywhere," he said. "Those trails and paths crisscross all over the hillside. It would be easy to get lost."

"Mr. Overstreet, you and your wife can help by looking in this area, directly above your house and to the left as you face uphill. Be sure to stay below the ridge." The deputies exchanged a glance. "Tom and I will get help and search up in the Forest Service area."

"Mr. Jones, perhaps you would join Mrs. Overstreet's sister and do the same. Search between the house and the ridge, but to the right. Again, please be sure to confine yourselves to this slope."

Dad coughed. "Perhaps Mr. Jones had better join me. My wife's sister isn't feeling very sympathetic toward the Joneses right now."

So it was decided. Mom and Aunt Ruth would search right, Dad and Mr. Jones would search left. The deputies would concentrate between the two houses and above the ridge. I would stay with Corky.

When we got to Corky's house, Mom went to find Aunt Ruth, and I looked for Corky. He was in the garage, holding a big hammer. A brown paper bag lay on the hard floor. Merlin bustled around the room, investigating corners and stacks of boxes. Now and then he sat back and scratched, or dashed up to Corky for a quick pat.

Bang! Corky brought the hammer down with all his strength. Then he turned the bag and hit it again.

Bang! He hardly looked up when I came in.

"What's that?"

"Bones."

Bang!

"What kind of bones? Did you finally find a dead squirrel?"

"Nope."

Bang!

"Come on, Corky. What kind of bones?"

"The best kind. Ghost bones."

Honestly!

He didn't want to show me and he didn't want to tell me, so I changed the subject.

"They're looking for Georgette."

He put the hammer down and looked at me searchingly. "I like her. And she didn't give me drugs. That was a magic plant and it wasn't drugs and she didn't give it to me anyway."

He took a deep breath. "I like her. She's like me."

"I like her too, Corky." Suddenly I realized how much I meant that. "But what do you mean, she's like you?"

"Just that we have a lot in common." Then, quietly, "Like she hasn't got a mom and I haven't got a dad."

Bang!

Corky always has an answer. Sometimes the answer makes a lot of sense.

Chapter 18

I left Corky to his magic and went into the kitchen. The wind still pestered the bushes, and the clouds glowered over the hill like angry giants.

"I hope we find Georgette before this storm breaks," I told Mom.

She and Aunt Ruth, wrapped in their warmest jackets, went out the back door and started up the hill. I settled in front of the television with my breakfast — a glass of milk and a peanut butter and jelly sandwich. An old science fiction movie was on, "Invasion of the Slimy Grapefruit" or something. Just as the slime was creeping up on a Beautiful Young Thing, the door opened, and Corky walked in with Merlin.

At first I didn't pay any attention to him. The slime was millimeters away from the Beautiful Young Thing. I took a bite of my sandwich and waited for the Blood-Chilling Scream.

"Ahemm!"

I looked at Corky. His forehead was smeared with dry reddish powder. I couldn't think of anything nice to say, so I ignored it.

95

"What's up?"

The BYT was screaming now.

"Just wondered if you saw me here," he said.

The invisibility spell. I should have caught on right away. I humored him.

"I see you, but maybe your edges are a little blurred. Of course, I've known you forever. To a stranger you might be just a smudge."

That really pleased him. He grinned, and I turned back to the slimy grapefruit.

It was sort of fun making him feel good. I decided to do it more often.

An hour later, just as the last grapefruit was defeated by the Brave Young Hero, a soft sound at the window drew my attention. Huge drops splattered on the glass. Somehow the drops outside made the house seem more warm and comforting.

Georgette had never been far from the surface of my mind. Now I could think of nothing else. Even if she had fallen in the dark and hurt herself, she should have been found by now. I called home, just in case they had found her and hadn't told me. No answer.

I went out to the garage. No Corky.

With the television off and the only sound the insistent raindrops, the house was suddenly too quiet. I felt a stab of alarm. Where was Corky?

Maybe there was something to his nonsense about ghosts and magic spells. I was beginning to feel cursed. People close to me kept disappearing! I ran through the house, calling his name.

Corky was gone.

I forced myself to stand quietly and think. Dad always told me that a minute of thought is worth an hour of action. So I tried it.

Corky liked Georgette. He said they were alike. Now Georgette was in trouble and Corky wanted to help, even though he was afraid of his ghosts on the hill.

He really believed his collection of magic charms would protect him. That would explain what he was doing with the "ghost bones." He must have smashed the clay voodoo doll and smeared the dust on himself in order to be invisible while he searched for Georgette.

I began to wish I hadn't encouraged him by telling him that his spell had worked. Smudge indeed!

That was enough thought. I scribbled a note.

> Corky has gone to find Georgette.
> I'm going to find Corky.

Then, as an afterthought, I wrote the time so they would know how long I had been gone.

> 10:00 A.M.

The rain washed across the windows in a solid sheet. I searched in Aunt Ruth's closet and found her old green vinyl raincoat, pulled it over my sweater, and dashed out the door.

The wind was moaning now, and the trees seemed like tormented spirits. The rain had settled into a steady downpour.

"Corky!"

The wind and rain covered my voice and kept it from going very far. Still, I tried again.

"Corky!"

He might have been gone for an hour already.

At least he had Merlin. I wished the little dog were a real magician. We needed one.

Up the hill I trudged. I didn't dare go too fast, for fear I might walk right past him. I pulled the jacket hood up. It kept the rain off my head, but it also blocked my view and muffled my ears. I had to turn from side to side to see and hear around me.

The ground had been hard and dry from the long drought, but with each step I felt it softening. I would leave a trail.

I passed the spot where Corky had found the charm. I passed the pocket mine. Nothing. I bent to search the underbrush. Perhaps I would find footprints, or even see Merlin dashing under the shrubs that blocked my way. As I bent and searched, a memory stirred. It had seemed insignificant at the time, but suddenly I saw it again, as if it were just now happening.

Corky and Merlin were walking through the manzanita thicket, Merlin doing his excitement-dance and Corky bending over — searching.

What had he picked up that day? Now I was sure I knew, and now I also knew that Georgette and Corky were not just lost. They were in danger.

Chapter 19

My first thought was to run home, to tell someone what I had figured out, but probably no one would be there. I had just as good a chance of finding one of the deputies up on the hill. Besides, Corky must be somewhere close, and I didn't dare leave him alone. He could be in awful danger.

"Corky!" I headed up the hill, shouting against the wind.

Corky must have figured it out, too. It wasn't ghosts that had him scared. He knew Georgette needed help as she faced a very human enemy.

I shouted again, but I was torn between hoping Corky would hear me and being afraid someone else would. The rain fell harder. It drummed on Aunt Ruth's jacket and the hood acted like a tin roof, magnifying the sound of each drop. I thrust my hands deep into the pockets and squinted against the wind.

There. To the left I saw a flash of white. I was at the crest of the hill now, just on the edge of the Forest Service land. Another flash of white. I tried to remember what Corky had been wearing and hoped desperately that he had put on some kind of coat.

Or maybe he thought being invisible was protection from rain, too.

I stumbled off the path toward the fluttering white object. Roots and rocks stuck out of the ground and low-hanging branches snatched at me. One yanked the hood back. When I tugged myself free, the overhanging branches dumped water down my neck.

Water ran into my eyes, partly blinding me, but I made my way to the trunk of a huge ponderosa pine. Its thick branches and long needles protected me from the downpour. I wiped my eyes and searched the surrounding forest. Not ten feet away, at the base of a fir tree, stood Corky's ghost. I gasped, then laughed out loud.

It was a scarecrow.

Someone had taken a tall bamboo pole and had draped an old sheet around the top. The head was stuffed and tied around the neck with a bit of rope, and the bottom edge was jagged and torn. It flapped and crackled in the brisk wind. It was easy to imagine Corky's terror as he was chased by someone waving this prop high overhead. It was bad enough in the daytime; it must have been horrible at dusk. I admired Corky's courage for coming back here at all.

I took a moment to catch my breath and consider the ghost. It all began to fit together. There had been poachers, all right, but they weren't after gold. They were after a crop of marijuana that someone had raised on the Forest Service land. They were probably kids — pretty easy to scare off with a giant "ghost" and a lot of noise from a siren.

And a few rifle shots. That's what really scared me. Whoever was willing to break the law by growing marijuana was also willing to use guns to protect it. I hated the idea that Corky was alone out here.

And Georgette.

Then I had another idea that I hated even more. What if Georgette was involved somehow? It would explain her heading up the hill when she left my party. Maybe she had been here before. Maybe she was the one who dropped the charm. I felt confused.

As I tried to sort through all the things I knew about Georgette, the wind caught the scarecrow and tumbled it to the ground. It looked silly and dirty and not at all like a terrifying banshee. I wished Corky could see it like this.

Corky. Once more I saw him in my imagination. He bent to the ground and picked up a sprig of something leafy, then stuffed it in his pocket.

It had been marijuana. He didn't recognize it. He only knew it was an unusual plant, something odd and worth saving. I didn't recognize it at first, either, two days ago when I snooped in Corky's collection of charms. But Aunt Ruth had. She just didn't know where it had come from.

Probably the poachers had dropped it, either carrying it down the hill across our land or in their panic that day when we saw them being chased away.

Aunt Ruth had assumed that Georgette had given it to him, but Corky had told us the truth when he said she hadn't. We had all figured that he was trying to protect Georgette; we hadn't given him a chance or a reason to explain.

Corky didn't always talk pollygobble.

The cold wet seeped through my shoes. My toes felt as though they belonged to someone else, and they didn't particularly like being along on this trip. I pushed away from the trunk of the friendly old pine and headed deeper into the woods.

I didn't call out any more. I walked as silently as I could, searching the woods for any sign of Corky and Merlin. By now the ground was wet enough so that they would be leaving tracks in the fresh mud.

I thought I heard something in the trees behind me, but when I turned around no one was in sight. Surely if it had been one of the deputies, he would have said something. I decided it must have been my imagination and refused to think about the possibility that it might have been a bear, or worse.

It wasn't easy going. Aside from the rain and wind and the rough footing, the ground started to slope steeply down on the left. I didn't remember ever being on this land before, but now I continued around the edge of the hill.

The wind faded, and the raindrops hit my face more gently, as I followed the deer trails around the curving slope. It was tricky in places. Deer have four feet, after all, and can maneuver across a hill too steep for a teenager, even one in tennis shoes. I discovered that the word "teenager" had developed a sour taste.

I must have hiked more than a mile when the hill curved right and leveled out. I had never been back this far. I was surprised to see that between the ridge above our house and the next high ridge behind it was a huge flat area. It was a miniature plain, dotted with tall pines and madrone. There was almost no undergrowth.

A flicker of movement caught my eye. Two men stood near the far edge of the clearing. They were too distant for me to see their faces clearly, but they wore wide-brimmed hats and plaid shirts. One had a bushy beard.

I ducked and peeked at them from behind a large outcrop of granite. One of the men bent over and tied ropes to one end of a kind of canvas sled. He attached them in a giant loop, like a handle. The bearded man stood beside a leafy plant that was almost as tall as he was. About a dozen similar plants grew in a row beside the first.

Marijuana! I was astonished at its size. No wonder they protected their crop. It was probably worth a fortune.

He stooped over and cut the plant's stalk nearly at ground level. The marijuana toppled. Working together, the two men harvested the remaining plants and heaped them on the canvas sled. Then each man slipped a shoulder into the rope handle, and they pulled together like a team of horses. Straining from the heavy load, they slowly made their way down a narrow trail that led from the far side of the field.

I had barely breathed as I watched them at work, and now my heart almost stopped. A voice came from behind me.

"I told you I was invisible. You walked right by me."

Chapter 20

"Corky!"

I was so glad to see him, I forgot to be quiet. I grabbed him and hugged him hard, and he squeaked. Merlin did a fancy four-step around our legs, but thank goodness he didn't bark.

Nothing about Corky looked glad. He was drenched, and the reddish powder on his face had turned to smears of mud. I was right: his ghost bones had been dried clay.

I crouched again and pulled him down beside me. Merlin crowded close, too, and the three of us huddled there, warming each other with our rain-wet bodies.

"You walked right past us back there," he said. "So we followed you to be sure you didn't get into any trouble."

I didn't smile. He was perfectly serious.

"Thank you. I thought you were mad at me because of the way I treated Georgette."

"Oh, you couldn't help that." If anything, he looked even more solemn. "Sometimes people just make mistakes."

He ducked his head and sniffed. A giant drop rolled down his nose, and for a moment I wasn't sure if it was rain or maybe a tear.

"Don't worry about her, Corky. They've probably found her by now."

He kept his head down, stubbornly refusing to look up at me. Merlin gazed into Corky's face and whined softly.

I tightened my hug, and suddenly Corky was crying on my shoulder. His sobs were eerily quiet, a muted wail. It was as though he was full of silent demons. He muffled the sound against his mother's jacket, and I thought how wrong it was for me, not her, to be holding him.

At last he quieted and mumbled, "It's the wrbn."

"What?"

"The rain," he whispered. "It's the rain."

"Corky, I don't understand. What about the rain?"

"It's like when my dad was killed. It was the rain."

Of course. It hadn't rained, at least rained hard, since that awful day last spring when Uncle Bill's truck went off the mountain road.

"I've been doing magic to keep the rain away," he said so softly that I had to lean even closer to hear. "It worked, too, until now. But now the rain is back, and it's going to get Georgette."

He shuddered. "I *hate* the rain."

In spite of his words, or maybe because he finally had a chance to say the words aloud, he was calmer,

107

but there was still a tenseness in his small body. Merlin licked his hands, as though in sympathy, and I kept my arm around his shoulders.

"Let's go home," I said softly. "Your mother will be worried, and we have a lot to tell our folks."

He pulled away. "No, we can't."

"We have to, Corky." I figured he hadn't seen the two men, and I hoped to get him out of there before he did.

"We can't leave now," he insisted. "Those men have Georgette."

I should have known.

"I think they're the same guys who were snooping around our house the other day. Pretending to be lost."

"How do you know they have Georgette?"

"I followed them. I heard them dragging something along that old logging road, so I sneaked through the brush to see what they were doing. There's an old pickup parked down there, and another guy, with a gun."

My worst suspicions surfaced one last time. "Was Georgette with them?"

"No. Not *with* them. They have her tied up. I was on my way for help."

I was relieved for an instant, then more scared than ever.

"I'm afraid they'll take her away. If they do, we'll never see her again." He took a swipe at his rain-drenched face with his sleeve. His eyes looked haunted.

I understood at last. His fear for Georgette was all mixed up with the rain and his father's death. He felt responsible — and helpless.

"Okay, I'll go and keep an eye on them. You go down and get help."

He muttered something under his breath, and I had to ask him to repeat it.

"I said I was lost!" He looked embarrassed. "I've never been up this far. When I tried to go for help, I couldn't figure out which way to go."

He shrugged impatiently. "I think I made a big circle."

I started to explain how to get home, but it was too complicated, and he looked too scared. It occurred to me that he could easily get lost again. Also, when I looked at his face, I realized that he didn't want to be alone.

"Let's go, then. But be sure Merlin is quiet."

Corky's shoulders straightened. His shock of red hair, plastered against his head like a little helmet, made him look like a comic soldier. Merlin jumped to his feet and wriggled wetly, but he didn't make a sound.

We peered around the rock. Not a movement, not a sign of life disturbed the sodden clearing.

We started off to our right, keeping in the wooded area at the edge of the open space. It was slow going because we had to climb over fallen logs and skirt dense thickets of manzanita and poison oak. At least the sound of the rain partly muffled our noise. I took comfort from the idea that no one was likely to be watching for us. No sane person would be out in the morass we had to climb through.

I glanced at my watch and gasped. It was past noon. We had been gone for over two hours.

I longed for home and warmth, and even Aunt Ruth's agonized anger. But then I thought of Georgette's face. Her eyes had been so full of pain, but instead of crying out, she had just drifted away from us. If I could help her, I must.

Finally we met the faint trail down which the two men had hauled the load of marijuana. The soft ground was streaked with skid marks left by the canvas sled. Tiny seedlings that had sprouted in the sunny path lay flattened.

The sound of a branch snapping made us both jump and, for the first time, Merlin growled low in his throat. No other sound followed, and we couldn't see anyone.

But we should see someone, I thought. Where are those deputies?

Wordlessly we crept back into the deeper forest and followed along beside the path. Then ahead we heard voices.

If they hadn't been talking, I don't know if we would have seen them before we stumbled into them. The truck was old, about as old as Dad's, but while his was freshly painted and cared for, this one was a wreck. The owners had evidently used cans of spray paint to give it a coat of miscellaneous green and brown splotches, like the camouflage paint used by the army. It wasn't pretty, but it worked. From a little distance the truck blended almost perfectly into the background of shrubs and trees.

Three men stood around the truck, the two I had seen before and one other, a huge man who wore a dark khaki slicker that made him seem even bigger. He was clean shaven, but his hair was long and pulled into a ponytail at the back. He nestled a rifle in the crook of his arm, tenderly, as though it were a child. As we watched, he leaned his huge bulk forward and spat a brownish stream onto the ground through a space in the front of his mouth that had once held a tooth. Now there was only a gaping hole. He dug into the poncho pocket and pulled out a plastic bag, reached in with his thumb and forefinger, and daintily pulled out a wad of tobacco, which he tucked between his lower lip and gum.

"There are our ghosts," I whispered to Corky, but he didn't answer. His gaze was fixed on the truck, or rather, under it.

There, muddy and miserable looking, lay Georgette.

Chapter 21

Her arms were twisted behind her back, and her wrists and ankles were bound by thick rope. She lay on her stomach beneath the truck, with her head turned toward us. Her mouth was bound by a wide red handkerchief. She gave no sign of having seen us in the underbrush.

Perhaps the men had put Georgette under the truck to protect her from the rain; it was drier down there. Even so, her hair was wet, her face was smeared with mud, and her glasses were missing. I wanted to think it was our good cover that kept her from seeing us, because that would mean the men might not notice us, either. But I was afraid the missing glasses were the real reason.

"It took all night and most of today, but I think we have it all." The bearded man swung the last plant from the canvas sled into the truck. He took off his hat and wiped his forehead with the back of his right arm. He sighed and leaned against the truck.

"These blasted high school kids have messed with us once too often," the man with the gun said. "They've been in our hair and stealin' our crop for almost a month, and now this one has seen us." He interrupted himself to spit on the ground in the general direction of Georgette. "I say it's time to teach the little sneaks a lesson."

I crouched lower and peered between his feet at Georgette's wretched face. She was right to be scared. These guys must have been the ones who were shooting that day, and now I was sure that they really had been shooting *at* us. I reached out and pulled Corky closer. He in turn held Merlin, one hand lightly around the little dog's muzzle.

"Aww, Mike, why not just leave her up here? She's more like a scared rabbit than anything." The bearded man bent his head slightly so the brim of his hat protected a match flame he held to the end of his cigarette. He took a deep drag and tossed the match carelessly to the ground.

Thank goodness it's raining, I thought. Yesterday the whole hill, including our house, would have been in flames. The idea made me so angry, I almost forgot to be scared.

"Dave, I've had enough of you, too. It was your damn stupid idea to use a scarecrow and those sirens. That sure didn't keep the little poachers out." He actually sounded offended at the idea that someone would steal from him! "Now we'll try it my way. She goes with us."

My heart sank. That was exactly what Corky had been afraid of. I felt helpless as we watched them get ready to leave. The man with the missing tooth held his gun on Georgette, while the other two grabbed her arms and dragged her, face in the mud, out from under the truck. One took her ankles, and they swung her up into the pickup bed. She landed awkwardly, but the piles of cut marijuana cushioned her fall.

They used the canvas tarp to cover both the marijuana and Georgette. Then they fastened it down with ropes. The three of them climbed into the cab. The engine sputtered, wheezed into life, then settled into an uneven, rasping moan.

I can't exactly explain my reasons for what I did next. Maybe I did it because I'm impulsive. That gets me into trouble often enough. I wish I had acted because I am an Independent Thinker, but I'm not so sure I did. Mostly I wasn't thinking clearly at all, I was so scared and angry. Maybe, as they said later, I'm brave. But I certainly didn't feel brave. I only knew that I couldn't let them leave with Georgette.

"You and Merlin will have to go for help," I told Corky. "Just keep heading downhill. You can't get too lost."

"I want to help her get away," he muttered.

"Then get help," I repeated and, before I dared to think about it any more, I ran from the brush, jumped on the rear bumper, and scrambled under the tarp.

Georgette squealed in terror as I reached for her. In the dark, and without her glasses, she couldn't tell what was happening.

114

"It's me," I whispered. "Jess."

Her muffled voice managed to let me know she was glad to see me, even though the words were lost in the gag. Then I felt the truck begin to move. I fumbled at the knots in the handkerchief and finally tore it from her mouth.

"Jess, I was so scared." Her voice was as thick as mud as she tried to make her tongue and lips behave. The words came slowly, but each one was clearer than the one before.

"I still *am* scared."

I spoke close to her ear. Although the lurching and the roar of the truck made it hard to be heard, I was still afraid to shout.

"Roll over so I can cut the ropes."

I dug in my pocket for the little knife, pulled it open, and tucked it under the ropes that bound her hands. The truck jerked wildly, and I could hear one of the men swear. Then the rear wheels spun, whined, and took hold, and we jumped forward again. I felt the ropes give way under the sharp blade, and then piercing pain followed as the tip caught the base of my left thumb.

Georgette rubbed her sore wrists, and I dove for her feet, vowing to be more careful. The truck stopped suddenly, then reversed with a loud grinding of gears. Then, with more whining from the tires, it swung in a tight circle to head down the road toward the highway. I had to hurry!

I hacked desperately at the ropes around her ankles as the truck lurched down the road. Just as the last fiber burst, the pickup slammed to a stop, and the knife slipped. I stifled a screech as the tip once more hit my thumb. With my right hand, I closed the blade and stuffed the knife back in my pocket.

A grating sound told me that the driver had set the emergency brake, then voices rang out.

Georgette and I cringed and wriggled down into the leafy bed. We were sure we'd see the cover ripped from the truck and a gun barrel pointed directly at us.

But that didn't happen. I winced when I heard someone shout, "There he goes! Get him!"

It must be Corky.

A shot rang out, followed by wild yelping. Merlin.

"Come on!" I shouted and grabbed Georgette's sore wrist. I half-pulled her to the tailgate, peered out, then ducked out from under the tarp and tumbled to the ground. Georgette followed as well as she could, but she slipped on the rear bumper and landed on me.

"Ugggh."

"I'm sorry, Jess."

I had no breath to answer. Another shot and more shouts urged me to my feet. I dragged Georgette into the underbrush beside the road.

In the distance I saw the three men, two of them waving guns, lumbering up the trail. In front of them raced Corky's small figure. He had taken off his jacket and was waving it over his head like a flag.

116

It flapped like a wet towel on a clothesline. In front of him, still yelping in outraged terror, ran Merlin.

"Run, Corky!" The men didn't hear my shout over their own noise and Merlin's, but Georgette grabbed my arm fiercely.

"What is it?" She sounded panicky, and I realized that she couldn't see the wild chase led by the spunky black dog.

"They're after Corky and Merlin. I've got to do something."

But what? I looked at the truck stopped in the middle of the narrow road at the top of a steep slope. If Corky could create a diversion for us, maybe, just maybe, I could do the same for him. Surely their marijuana would be more important to them than Corky.

"Get ready to run when I get back."

I dashed across the small area, yanked the passenger door open, and threw myself across the seat. My right hand groped wildly for the emergency brake release, and I hoped this truck really was like Dad's. Thank goodness the handle was there, right where I expected it. I pulled myself into the driver's seat and braced my foot against the dashboard.

Another shot rang out. Snatching my knife from my pocket, I flicked the blade open. I jammed the blade into the edge of the horn disc and at the same time squeezed the brake-release handle hard with my sore left hand and pulled back with all my strength. The handle popped free, and the truck

117

slowly began to roll. I pushed down on the horn and wedged the knife in tightly. The horn blared and kept on blaring.

A lot was going on, but I noticed a glitter out of the corner of my eye as the truck started to sway and bounce. The key was in the ignition, and hanging from it was a bit of broken chain, just like the piece on the charm Corky had found. I hoped the men really had run out of luck.

I tore open the driver's door and slipped to the ground as the truck wobbled and jerked down the logging road, picking up speed. All the while, the horn blared.

I dashed across the road, grabbed Georgette's wrist, and together we crashed off into the bushes. She lagged behind just a little because she couldn't clearly see the branches and roots that blocked our way, but she stumbled along gamely.

The men's shouts told me that they had turned to follow the truck, which charged down the road like an enraged bull. The horn bellowed, and the branches cracked like gunfire under the heavy tires. Shouts of outrage turned to alarm as the men began to realize that their precious crop was leaving without them.

"Corky's getting away," I yelled to Georgette.

Indeed, I could make out his form through the trees, improving his distance from the drug dealers with each leap. Merlin proceeded with confidence. Evidently he had known the way home all along.

Corky and Merlin were nearing a bend where they would soon be out of sight. But before they reached it, a figure stepped onto the path in front of them. He scooped up the little dog with one arm, and I watched in horror as he put out his other hand to grab Corky's shoulder.

I started to shout to distract him, when a second figure appeared right in front of Georgette and me. I tried to dodge, too late, and ran full tilt into him. Georgette completed the catastrophe by running full tilt into me.

Firm hands grasped my shoulders, too. I struggled to get free, twisting and using my elbows to try to break his grip. Finally I realized that the man was talking to me.

"Jessica, it's okay. Settle down. It's okay."

I stopped struggling and looked up into the face of Kevin Mulloy.

Now the woods seemed to be full of uniformed men. Another forest ranger stood beside Georgette.

The ground shook, and we heard a tremendous crash as the truck came to rest against an immense pine tree. Even so, the three men would never catch their truck. They stood in the middle of the road with their hands in the air. Four deputy sheriffs with drawn guns surrounded them.

Two more deputies joined the man who held Corky. One carried Merlin gently, and the other two, with Corky safely between them, waved reassurance as they walked toward us. By the time they reached us, Corky was actually grinning.

He showed us where the bullet had grazed Merlin's little rump. The pup would sit down cautiously for a while, but he was mostly scared.

I could understand that!

Within half an hour we were down the hill and home, being fussed over and cuddled, and basking in our roles as heroes.

I wasn't sure how we got that status, but for the time being it was just fine with me.

Georgette's dad was so relieved to see her that he cried. So did Mom.

Aunt Ruth listened intently as I told about how brave and sensible Corky had been, and how he had distracted the drug dealers in order to give Georgette and me a chance to get away. Finally she gave him one gentle kiss, which he did *not* draw away from, and told him that she could see he was growing up and she was very proud of him.

Mom and Dad looked alternately proud and terrified when I told them about getting into the truck to try to help Georgette. I felt alternately proud and terrified myself, come to think of it.

Kevin Mulloy returned my knife to me and declared that I was the bravest and most resourceful teenager he knew. I think he really meant it.

He also said I could call him Kevin.

We all had hot showers — I sure prefer warm and

wet to *cold* and wet — and changed into dry clothes. I lent Georgette a pair of jeans, and they were just a little too short for her. I had never realized before that she was almost my size. My blouse fit her perfectly.

Dad said I was an Independent Thinker *and* a Brave Girl. Mom bandaged my thumb. Aunt Ruth talked soothingly to Merlin as she took care of his sore backside.

Dad's eyes twinkled when he told Corky, "What you saw turned out to be pollygoblins."

Then it was time for the first hot chocolate of the season. We all gathered in the kitchen to hear Mr. Mulloy — Kevin — and the two deputies who had been at our house that morning tell their stories.

Kevin went first. After Dad had talked to him about the intruders on our hillside and had shown him the charm, he decided to investigate. Working with the sheriff's office, he set up aerial surveillance; for days Kevin and the deputies searched the forest around our house. At last they found what they were looking for: a crop of mature marijuana plants.

The deputies had gone on foot to investigate two nights before. (I remembered the flashing lights. I hadn't imagined them after all.) They found that the marijuana growers had posted guards, since the crop was ready to be harvested.

The deputies figured that high school students had discovered a short cut across our land, had taken bags and cutters, and had stolen as many plants as they could carry.

So the streamers and clanking noises of our "ghosts" had been no more than plastic bags and pruning shears!

Since school had started, the houses on our hill were usually empty during the day. The thieves worked pretty steadily until the marijuana growers noticed their missing plants and set up traps that triggered the sirens. One of the men had tried to scare Corky by making noises and chasing him down the hill. But the real thieves didn't scare easily, so the drug growers turned to guns.

The sheriff's office wanted to catch the whole gang, so they watched and waited. They had planned the raid for today, but with Georgette missing, they were afraid to move in. The marijuana growers would be desperate, and if they had Georgette, they might make her a hostage.

The deputies looked a little sheepish when they admitted that they had deliberately tried to get my folks, Aunt Ruth, and Mr. Jones out of the way. They didn't want to endanger anyone, but they couldn't let on about the raid. So the searchers were sent as far from the marijuana patch as possible.

"Besides," one said, "we really hoped you would find Georgette."

Their plan had worked for Georgette's dad, my parents, and Aunt Ruth, but they hadn't counted on Corky and me. When we showed up, they couldn't move without endangering us further. They could only wait.

As soon as Georgette was free and Corky and Merlin were out of reach, the police had moved in.

Kevin laughed aloud when he described the truck hurtling down the road with its horn blowing and the three men chasing it, guns drawn.

"You'd think they were going to shoot the truck," he said with a chuckle. "But by then their luck was so bad, I doubt they could have hit it."

Chapter 22

"They'll be here any minute."

Tiff checked her new dress in the mirror for the twentieth time. I looked into the mirror too, and caught Georgette's eye. She giggled and put up her hand to cover her mouth.

But she didn't push her glasses back. In the six months since that awful day on the hill, her father had decided to get her contact lenses. He hadn't stopped there, either. He enlisted Mom and me, and we helped Georgette pick out a whole new wardrobe.

Tiff did her part by helping Georgette fix her light brown hair.

Mom and I had asked if we could give Georgette a party for her thirteenth birthday. It was about to begin.

The doorbell rang. Tiff shrieked and grabbed me. Georgette giggled again. We all trooped out to the living room, and Georgette opened the door.

Josh and Tim stood there, first as usual. They said hello to Tiff and me, but they never took their eyes off Georgette.

It was like that all night. Georgette danced. Georgette chattered with a whole group of boys around the stereo. Georgette helped Mom keep food on the table, and three boys helped Georgette.

"We don't need squirrel dust," I told Tiff. "We already are invisible." Tiff laughed ruefully.

The doorbell pealed. It was Aunt Ruth and Kevin Mulloy, delivering the evening's entertainment. Kevin had given Corky some lessons in what he called "real magic," and as a special present to Georgette, tonight was to be Corky's first official performance.

He stood straight and tall and wore a black cape and a little magician's top hat made for him by Aunt Ruth. At his heels, also wearing a tiny top hat, pranced Merlin.

They strutted across the room as Georgette clapped her hands for quiet. When everyone had settled down, Georgette made the introduction.

"Thank you all for the happiest birthday ever," she began. "I hope you will welcome a special guest, the world's greatest magician under the age of ten" — she paused to giggle — "and his special assistant, Merlin."

Everyone joined in the laughter and applauded politely, while Corky strutted to the center of the room. He cut a rope in half and magically joined it together. He asked Georgette to choose a card, then he picked the identical card out of a whole deck. He changed a king of hearts into a jack, then changed it back. And for his finale, he put Merlin into a box and changed him into a bouquet of flowers, which he presented to Georgette.

It was a brilliant performance, even though the box barked once after Merlin had vanished.

Corky was a hit. Josh and Tim whistled and stomped. Mr. Jones shouted "Bravo." Aunt Ruth looked proud.

I was proud, too — proud of Georgette, and Tiff, of Corky, and even of myself.

Tim wants to bring some gold pans over when the spring rains run in the gully again. I agreed right away. I don't know if we'll find gold, but it will be fun to look.

After all, everyone needs a little magic.